I Played Death

BY

Mark Hill

For these who experienced sever grief and these who, with the help of love, managed to overcome sadness. For these who love film and cinema.

"I played death"

Foreword:

This is a short story about Carol, a talented and well-known actress. After a terrible accident, in which her family are killed, she experiences severe grief which leads to paranoia and her retreat into a world of fantasy. Although her new world is not real, but more like a mirror reflecting perfect images, Carol finds that the images she sees in her dreams and fantasies start to become more real than reality for her. As the story continues, the borders between reality and fantasy become extremely narrow and hard to distinguish.

Mark Hill

I played death

Carol had spent some time in the Mirror Room. Its walls were covered with large cupboards, and tall mirrors were placed on the cupboard doors. Standing in the middle of the room, she found herself surrounded by mirrors on all sides. Hung in the closets were clothes she had worn in each of her films. The room was also a place for her to practice acting her future roles. She was beautiful and talented. She was also very passionate about her work, and with a lot of effort and dedication she had been able to find fame as a prominent actress. Her effort, however, sometimes bordered on obsession. She first started her career in theatre as a teenager, and after a while she was able to get into television and film. She had been nominated for various awards during her career and several times she had won. Years ago, she married Gerald, a young and talented writer and journalist, and they had two children, eight-year-old Peter and four-year-old Rose. Despite, or perhaps because of, her marriage to a reporter, she always tried as much as possible to avoid controversy and the harsh glare of the media. Now, after years of marriage to Gerald, she was known as a woman committed to her family and her art.

She did her best to bring herself to public attention through her art, not her private life. It was not easy. She loved her husband deeply and felt she somehow owed her fame and popularity to his empathy. He was a man who patiently tried to help her in every moment of their life together, and he was a good father to their children.

Her soul was inspired by the most recent script she had read. She found the script so compelling, she immediately agreed to play the part of a woman with cancer. But it would still be a long time before the film was shot. She intended to prepare herself thoroughly for the part and had read the script repeatedly. Now she carried the subject of the film, and the role she had to play, inside her at all times.

For some time now, she had prepared for the role by working two days a week in a hospital cancer ward. Of course, she did it in such a way that the news of her job did not reach the media. Only one of the nurses and the doctor in charge knew who she really was. The job was mainly supervisory but still involved carrying out some of the basic tasks of an orderly nurse, befriending patients who were close to death.

Among the patients was a woman about her own age who was suffering from advanced stage brain cancer. That night in the Mirror Room she tried to remember the facial expressions of the woman; the way she spoke and suffered; her hopes and aspirations. When Carol left the room, she felt an immense grief, as if she herself was sick with cancer.

She swore and said to herself, "Oh, I have brought my obsession and my madness into the family home again." When she reached the door of her children's rooms, a feeling of deep love and affection overwhelmed her. She entered their rooms and kissed their cheeks as they slept. Forgetting her earlier grief, she now felt happy and blessed.

She entered her own bedroom and found Gerald reading a book. She lay down beside him and, without permission, grabbed the book and threw it into a corner.

She pulled Gerald close, rested her head on his chest and said, "You don't know how lucky we are." She hugged him tighter and fell silent.

Aware she was preparing for a new role; Gerald smiled and kissed the top of her head. "Darling, you are very hard on yourself. I am proud of your talent and hard work, and I have never met anyone as dedicated to their work as you," he said. "But you must also take care of yourself. Your life does not just belong to you; I need you and so do the children. You are right that we are very lucky. I have a job I love, and you are more successful than ever. Most importantly, we have two beautiful children, and we should enjoy watching them as they grow up. I am a very lucky man, and you are the main reason for my happiness. Now try to rest a little. Do you have to work in the hospital again tomorrow?"

"Yes"

"If going there upsets you, don't go. Or at least spend less time there."

Carol raised her head from Gerald's chest and stared into his eyes. After a while, she said, "I'm sorry if my work has affected you and the children again."

"We just don't want to see you sad and worried. I know that behind those feelings there is creativity and humanity, but slow down."

Carol kissed Gerald and said: "I love you."

"Now, you'd better rest a little. Are you sure you have to go to the hospital again in the morning?"

"Yes, but the good thing is that I can at least safely carry out my work. The news hasn't been leaked anywhere."

***

Early in the morning she left her bedroom and went to the kitchen. The housekeeper, Sandra, was preparing breakfast. When Sandra saw Carol, she greeted her and said, "Are you going to the hospital? I have prepared breakfast."

"No, thank you. I don't have time for breakfast. Please tell Roger to get ready as soon as possible."

Sandra left the kitchen and returned a few moments later with Roger, Carol's driver and bodyguard of many years.

"I drove around the neighbourhood a while ago to make sure no one was around," Roger said.

"Okay, we better go soon, particularly since you have to come back here to get the kids to school." She had arranged to travel to the hospital in a way that would not attract attention. First, she was going with Roger to the house of an actress friend. There, after changing her clothes and putting on a wig, she would leave through the back door and drive herself in an old car to the hospital. When they reached her friend's house, she said goodbye to Roger and rang the doorbell. A few moments later, the maid opened the door, and she went inside.

Her friend had given her a room in the house where she could change her clothes. To reach the room she had to pass through the living room, where several bottles of wine and a half empty glass were on the table.

Seeing the drinks, Carol turned to the maid and said, "It seems Gloria had a drink last night."

The maid immediately began to clean the table and after a few moments said, "This didn't just happen last night."

Carol frowned and asked: "What do you mean?"

The maid stopped cleaning and said, "I know you are a close friend of Mrs. Gloria, and I don't like to interfere in her private affairs. I have been working for her for many years and I love her. But for some time now she has been drinking a lot. Please talk to her. She is often very sad. Just don't say anything about this conversation or it will only upset her further."

Carol shook her head and said, "Don't worry, I won't tell her."

At that moment, Gloria hurried out of her bedroom in her pyjamas and went to the bathroom, where she started to vomit loudly. The maid just stared at Carol and left.

Carol hurried to the bathroom door and said sadly, "Hey Gloria, how are you?"

After coughing several times, Gloria said in a hushed voice, "Yeah, don't worry. I think I drank a little too much last night."

"I'm making coffee now."

"Don't bother yourself too much."

"No, I want a coffee myself. I haven't eaten breakfast yet."

After a while, Carol returned to the room with two cups of coffee and saw Gloria sitting on a chair with dishevelled hair and puffy eyes. After placing the cups on the table, she turned to Gloria and said, "You don't seem well."

"I'm not too bad. I think I'll feel better after drinking this coffee." She drank a few sips and looked at Carol. "I'm sorry you have to see me like this. For years, I used to tidy myself up before leaving the bedroom. I never wanted anyone to see me in this state. Even my ex-husbands never saw me looking like this, but now it doesn't make any difference to me."

Carol stared at her with concern. "What happened? Why are you so sad?"

Smiling bitterly, Gloria said, "What more do you think should happen? A few months ago, I divorced my third husband, and my work has been in decline for years. What else did you think had gone wrong? You have seen the newspapers and heard about my divorce. My life has been in a downward spiral for a long time now and I don't think I'll ever regain the fame I used to have. You know better than anyone how this feels."

"No, you are wrong. You are still an attractive woman, and you are the same talented, popular actress you always have been."

Gloria smiled bitterly again and said, "It seems you need glasses! Look at my face. What beauty are you talking about? As for my acting, I haven't been offered a good role for years. What popularity are you talking about? I know you are my friend, but please don't lie to me or yourself."

"I'm not lying. If I have succeeded as an actor, it was partly because of our friendship and your advice. You have always tried to help and guide me, ever since I was a novice."

Gloria calmly replied, "Your success is down to your talent and hard work. Of course, we all need luck, but your main strength is your dedication and love for our profession."

"Don't you love acting?"

"Yes, but I always loved the fame and prestige that came with the job more than the art of acting. My ultimate goal was fame and influence and for a while, I had that. I'm not saying I hated the job or wasn't talented. Everyone who reaches our level has some talent, but the question is what do they want to achieve with their talent?"

"Even if you have gone through all of this for the sake of fame, you haven't done anything wrong. Most people, especially in our profession, are looking for fame and popularity. I don't think that's a bad thing."

"I didn't say it's bad, but it's not enough. Do you know what the difference is between you and me? You work for the art and to grow as a person, even if you also enjoy the fame. I've only been looking for more fame, which is why I have acted in so many awful films, movies that I knew were nothing more than shit as soon as I started working on them."

"But many actors do that to survive. I don't mean just to earn the money to survive, I mean to stay active to survive. A lot of the time they are the only roles we are offered."

"But since I became famous, I have had the chance to choose

and not taken it."

"But you have acted in a lot of beautiful films."

"Yes, but I was not the main reason those films were good; the writers, directors and producers were."

"You are lying to yourself now. I know that in this profession opportunities for women of our age are limited, but that shouldn't make you doubt yourself."

Gloria laughed. "Limited? That's putting it optimistically! There might be some truth to what you say, but the reality for women is that there are only a handful of us who can stay in this profession for a long time. For men it's different even 100-year-old bastards are offered major roles. Now let me give you some advice, you should get ready for your decline. It's a bitter thought but prepare yourself because it's the reality."

Carol smiled. "As long as I have a part to play, I don't care what it is. I would even enjoy playing in an anonymous little theatre."

Gloria shook her head. "So now you have admitted it! The difference between you and me is that you love art. That is why you are going to that hospital to visit those dying people. I would never do that! Honestly, even when I got involved with charities it was only to attract praise from others. Even recently, I deliberately planted negative stories about myself in the press just to get attention. I'll do anything to try and attract attention, but even the negative stories don't always work now. I have been a failure for a long time."

"You shouldn't think like that. You have done a lot in this job, both for yourself and for the profession."

Gloria smiled. "Enough about me. I hope you get that award you have been nominated for again."

"Thank you, I have to go now but we should spend more time together soon."

"Don't worry, I'm not going to commit suicide."

"I know, but we are friends, and we should help each other. I have never forgotten all the help you have given me."

"Yes, you're right, especially as our friendship will make me more famous!"

Carol laughed. "Oh, shut up."

"I'm just telling you the truth."

"I have to go, but contact me whenever you feel lonely or upset."

Carol left the room to get changed for the hospital.

***

The corridors of the hospital were usually full of patients and staff. First, Carol had to go and see the nurse in charge of the cancer ward. The nurse, Christine, and one of the doctors were the only ones who knew Carol's true identity.

When she entered Christine's office, she saw her drinking coffee in a hurry while talking on the phone. A few moments later, Christine smiled and turned to Carol. "Oh, you are very serious about your job."

Carol smiled and said: "Not as serious as you. I want to thank you again. You are doing me a great favour by allowing me to work here and keeping it a secret."

Christine replied with the same smile, "Oh my God, you don't know how happy I am to have you here. I've often wanted to tell others who you are but, in the end, I've always managed to control myself. Just remember, when your work here is over, and you star in a movie about people with cancer I will tell everyone that you were here with me as a friend and a colleague."

"Okay, but please keep our secret until then. I want to spend more time here and I particularly want to get closer to Mary. How is she?"

Christine shook her head and said, "Not good. She underwent radiology and chemotherapy again yesterday. I was just about to go and see her. You'd better come with me."

They both went to Mary's room. She was lying on her bed, staring out of the window. Christine smiled and said, "Hey Mary, how are you? Carol came to see you again; she wants to spend more time with you." Carol went to Mary's bed and held her hand. "What would you like us to do today? Do you want me to take you outside? The weather is good."

Mary shook her head and said, "I'm not feeling well."

"Are you in pain?" asked Christine.

"Yes."

Christine injected her with some painkillers. "You'll be fine in a few moments. I'll leave you alone with Carol. I have to go and see other patients."

Carol stared at Mary's face, not knowing what to say or do. She decided to wait for the painkiller to work. As Mary closed her eyes, Carol tried to imagine what she was feeling. After a few minutes Mary opened her eyes and started vomiting.

Carol didn't know what to do, so she summoned a nurse. Soon Christine came back. Before long, the room smelt of vomit and mucus as Mary struggled to compose herself.

Looking on, Carol began to feel light-headed. "Go to my office and wait there," said Christine.

"But I can help you."

"We don't need your help. You'd better go."

Carol left and went to Christine's office, where she sat down on a chair and covered her face with her hands. After a while, Christine came to see her and said, "I don't blame you if you are not feeling well. It is not easy to see her in that condition. Let me bring you a drink."

"No, thank you. I can't drink anything."

"Have you eaten breakfast?"

"No, because I was afraid, I would feel nauseous when I came here."

"Don't be so upset. You will get used to this if you keep coming here."

"I have a lot of respect for what you and your colleagues are doing. I know how difficult your work is. Unfortunately, society doesn't value you as much as it should."

Christine smiled and said, "You understand the situation of the hospital. Thank you for being here and sympathising with us. No wonder you have become such a good actor. Now you better go outside for some fresh air. You can see Mary again in an hour or two."

Carol sat on a bench outside, watching the staff and patients as they came and went. After a while she went to see Mary again. There was less pain in Mary's face now, but a shroud of death still seemed to cover her whole face and body. Carol made an effort to smile. Softening her voice, she said "How are you? Are you still in pain?"

"No, I am not in pain now, but I am sure the pain will return soon." Then she laughed bitterly. "Don't worry, I am used to it."

"Christine told me that you underwent radiology and chemotherapy yesterday. I hope the treatment will be effective. At least it means you still have hope."

"Yes, if I didn't have hope, I would not have accepted treatment. Chemotherapy is very difficult. Hair loss isn't the only side-effect."

"I am sure that you are strong enough to overcome these difficulties and see your family again. How many children do you have?"

"Two: a girl and a boy. My son is 10 and my daughter is 6."

"Oh, great. I also have a daughter and a son."

After staring at Carol for a moment, Mary asked, "What do you really do here? Are you a nurse too?"

"No, I'm not a nurse. I just come here to see patients and try to help them, but I can't do much. Maybe I can help just by talking to them."

"Interesting. Do you do it out of kindness or for another reason?"

"What other reason could there be?"

"Some people help with charities because they lost a loved one to cancer. Have you?"

"No."

"So, you are looking for death, aren't you?"

"What? Searching for death?"

"Yes. All the patients in this ward are suffering from cancer and most of them are beyond saving. Haven't you seen the face of death yet?"

Carol frowned. "We'd better not talk about death; let's talk about life."

"Oh, talking about life is easy for you. But for me, and others like me, it's different. I don't want to say that I have given up on life but having this disease and being in this environment means my soul and body feel they are gradually being consumed by death. That's why I said you must be looking for death."

Carol was silent for a while, then said, "I think you are a very perceptive person. What was your job?"

"I was a teacher."

"That explains it."

"No, I wasn't perceptive enough to know about death when I was teaching. It was only after I got sick and came to hospital that I began to know about death. What is your job?

Carol was silent for a while, then replied, "I am an actor."

Mary smiled. "So, I was right that you are looking for death, but it's for a part, isn't it?"

"Playing death? What an interesting idea. You think like an artist."

"I love reading and I love movies and plays. The first time I saw you, your face seemed familiar, but I couldn't remember where I had seen you. Now I think I know who you are. Oh my God, perhaps I was meant to get cancer so I could talk to a great actor like you!"

Carol smiled, "Just promise, you won't tell anyone. If the news is leaked it will be difficult for me to come here. I would like to be able to continue to see you and others like you."

"So, you want to play death?"

"No, why are you talking about death? I want to learn to live in the kind of difficult situation you are in. But of course, in the future I am going to play a role in a movie as a woman suffering from cancer. "

"What happens to the woman in that movie? Will she die?"

Carol looked at Mary and said, "If I tell you the end of the story, it will lose its charm. In the future, when the film is shown and released, you can see the fate of that woman. Look, now it's better not to talk about death and movies. The weather is good would you like me to take you outside?"

"Yes, now I feel better. You must be one of those actors who believes in method acting."

"Yes, researching the character I am going to play always

helps me, although it takes up a lot of my time and energy. But in general, it helps make the characters I play more realistic. Now I think we should stop talking about my job and go outside."

***

That night, after putting her children to bed, Carol went to the Mirror Room to think for a while. She wanted to put herself in Mary's place and think about her illness. She stared at her face in one of the mirrors, trying to recall Mary's facial expressions when she was in pain or grieving, while going over the script in her mind. Ever since she had first read the script, she had felt immersed in it and the role was now part of her life. Even when she was asleep, part of her was struggling to find a better way to portray the character. Now in the Mirror Room, she tried to combine the script with the experience she had gained in the hospital.

She didn't know how long she had been in the room before the sound of knocking on the door brought her to her senses. Gerald knew she was lost in the role of her character and came to take her to their bedroom to rest. When Gerald entered the Mirror Room, Carol was surprised.

"What time is it?" she asked.

Gerald looked at his watch. "One in the morning. You have been in this room for hours and you were in the hospital all day. You must be very tired. Now you should come with me." Carol went to the bedroom and lay down on the bed.

Gerald stared anxiously at her and said, "You look sad and tired."

Carol told him about Mary: "She was in a lot of pain, and she was upset."

"Well. try to forget about the disease and the hospital and rest a little. You will make yourself sick like this. I think we need a break; you were in your previous film role until last month, and then immediately you started thinking about your next role."

Carol stared at Gerald in disgust. After a while she calmed down and apologised. "I'm sorry. I've cursed you and the kids with this damn thing."

"No, don't worry about me or the children. You have to take care of your health."

"Yes, you are right. We need a holiday. In two weeks, I have to go to that awards ceremony, but after that we will go on holiday. Maybe we can go skiing like last year. What do you think?"

"Yes, I can't think of a better idea. Just don't be too hard on yourself. I know that even on holiday you will think about your new role, but a change of scenery will be good for everyone. Now you better rest a little."

***

That night, Carol and Gerald went to an award ceremony for actors and filmmakers. Carol, in a beautiful dress with understated make-up, had a special charm. As usual, she had several short interviews with reporters before the ceremony began, and then she and Gerald went into the hall and sat down. After a while, it was time to introduce the award for Best Actress in a Leading Role. The person who was to announce the award was a famous man who had acted and directed in many films. He first introduced the nominees for the award and short clips of each of their films were screened.

He then opened the envelope he was holding and said Carol's name with a smile on his face.

Carroll kissed Gerald passionately and then went to the stage, but before she could reach the microphone, the same man who had introduced her said: "You have a few moments to overcome your excitement. I have to say something about you to this audience," Then he turned to the audience and said: " Over the years, I have had the honour of acting alongside Carol several times, and I have twice directed her. I must admit, I have never seen an actor with such talent, and such hard work and determination, meeting her has been one of my honours in this profession. Tonight, she deserves this award, and I hope we will see her art for many more years."

Then turned to Carol and said: "Come on," and stepped away from the microphone so that Carol could speak.

Carol spoke with great enthusiasm, first thanking her husband and family for their help, and then thanking the crowd and organizers. After the official end of the ceremony, a party was held in another hall, during which the actors and those involved in the cinema spent time together, while reporters interviewed the award winners. It was also a good time to talk to friends and acquaintances.

During the party, Carol again conducted several short interviews with reporters and was always surrounded by friends and acquaintances, each congratulating her on her success.

Richard, who was also a successful director, had been staring at Carol, looking for an opportunity to talk to her alone for a while. Finally, he took the opportunity to meet Carol and greeted her with enthusiasm and happiness. Carol looked at him in surprise for a moment, unable to believe that he was there that night .She walked over to him, and they hugged briefly.

"I didn't know you were here tonight!" Carol said excitedly. "I haven't heard from you in a long time. Are you still working hard?"

"Yes, I'm working on a big project right now. I think you really deserved this award; I am very happy to see your success and I sincerely congratulate you."

"Tonight, on stage, I should have mentioned you and thanked you in public," Carol said kindly. "I owe my situation today to your help, I haven't forgotten that many years ago you agreed to cast me in a prominent role that film was a turning point in my artistic and professional life. If it was not for that film, maybe no one would have heard my name until now."

"No, you are wrong, of course, the first big job in the life of any actor plays an important role, but with your talent and hard work sooner or later you would find your way in. Working with you has also made me proud, you know very well how I feel about you."

Carol stared at Richard sadly and said after a while: "I have not heard from you for a long time, the only news I received through the newspapers was the news of your divorce. I am very sorry. As a friend, I wanted to be by your side, but the problem is that you just don't want my friendship."

"Why not? Your friendship is so valuable to me."

"You know exactly what I'm saying, I love my husband, I am very happy to be with him, the reason I stay away from you is that I don't want to upset you. I'm sorry for what happened between us. That was years ago and, as I said, I love my husband."

"Yes, I understand that well and I wish you more success. You must be working on another project again, right? With the knowledge I have of you, you can't be inactive for long."

"Yes, I received a good script, and I accepted a new role."

"You and I will have to work together again in the future." Carol smiled and said: "It's as if you're not giving up! I'd better go now to find my husband, I do not want any rumours about me to start," and then said goodbye to Richard.

***

Several days later, she and her husband and children arrived by plane at an airport near where they were going on holiday. The day before, Sandra and Roger had gone to a hilltop villa to prepare for their arrival. When the plane landed, Roger was waiting for them at the airport with a car. They all got in the car happily and drove to the villa. Heavy snow covered all the mountains and hills. "Fortunately, this is a good, quiet place and like last year I don't think we're going to face any problems." Roger said during the drive.

On the way, everyone stared with pleasure and longing at the beautiful and majestic surroundings. After a while they arrived home; Carol, as soon as she got out of the car, threw a snowball at Gerald, and then they all started playing and throwing snow at each other. The beauty of nature brought passion and vitality in their souls.

After a while, they took the children back to the villa and handed them over to Sandra, and Carol and Gerald spent some time walking around. Carol, with all her being and emotions, loved the beauty of nature, knowing that the experience of those beauties would not only fill her existence with joy in that moment, but would also enrich her work in the future. Gerald was right when he said that even in those moments, she would be thinking about improving her work.

After a short walk, they returned home for dinner. Carol got the children ready for bed right after dinner. The children were tired because of the trip and the snowball fight they had. As the house was not very big, both children had to sleep in the same room. There were two beds in their bedroom, spaced apart. After the children got into their beds, Carol sat on the floor between the two beds, and Rose as usual, with her beautiful eyes, asked Carol to tell a story.

Carol thought for a moment and said: "Because you are both tired, I will only tell you a short story." Then she got closer to Rose's bed and said: "Did you know that in this area sometimes a caravan of joy passes?"

Rose asked with excited eyes: "What is a caravan of joy ?!"

Carol smiled and said: "The caravan of joy is a caravan made up of several carriages, each of which is drawn by beautiful horses. Those beautiful horses and carriages follow each other, and on their way, they visit all good children and take them to the city of happiness."

Rose asked again in surprise: "What is the city of happiness?"

"Oh, it is a city where there are all kinds of toys, and all good children can play there as much as they want."

"Is there a carousel there too, a small carousel, because I'm still afraid to ride big carousels?"

"Yes baby, there are all kinds of toys."

"Where does this caravan of happiness come from?"

Carol pointed to the window with a smile on her face and said: "Behind those mountains."

Rose asked in surprise again, "How are the horses able to cross the mountains?"

"Those chariots and horses are all magical and able to fly."

"So, they fly like Santa?"

"Yes darling."

A few moments later she looked serious and said: "Listen well, don't you hear the sound of horses' feet?"

Rose and Peter listened carefully for a while and after a few moments they both shook their heads.

"Listen carefully," Carol said again, and at the same time she turned to Peter and winked, and then struck one of her hands on the wood-covered floor, making the sound of horse's hooves. Peter, who knew that his mother was playing a role, smiled.

Rose said excitedly, "Oh, I hear the footsteps of the horses," and then she stared out the window and said: "They will pass over our heads now."

After a while, Carol stopped hitting the ground and kindly told Rose: "They're not going over our heads tonight."

"Why?! We were good children today."

"Yes, but we still have to do something else."

"What?"

"Oh, I have to tell you one more thing about those carriages."

"What?"

"The drivers of those carriages are snowmen that must first be made by good children and their parents. When a snowman is made, a carriage with beautiful horses will be given to those children and that snowman, along with the other carriages, will take the children and their parents to the city of happiness. Tomorrow we must make a beautiful and strong snowman and then wait for the caravan of joy, maybe it will pass over our heads in a few days. Now you'd better go to sleep, we have a lot of work to do tomorrow, making a snowman is not an easy task."

Then she kissed Rose and Peter, said good night to them and left the room.

***

The next day, Gerald and the children made a big snowman in front of the house, and then they all went to a ski slope where Gerald and Peter skied. In the evening, they returned home to

33

eat some food and rest a little. While they were eating, Carol's mobile phone rang, and Carol went to another room to answer it. After a while, Carol came back with a sad and confused expression. Seeing Carrol's upset face, Gerald immediately asked: "What happened? Is it bad news?"

"I'm sorry, I have bad news for you, I have to go to another city for a few days," Carol nodded sadly.

Gerald asked in surprise: "Where?"

"The last movie I was in had a problem and I have to go back to filming again. I'm very sorry, I have no choice but to go there," Carol said sadly.

"Don't they know you're on holiday?" Gerald replied angrily. "They should wait a few weeks and then you can go there."

Carol shook her head sadly and said: "No, they can't suspend all those people and facilities just for me; sorry, I have to go but I promise to join you again in a few days. I will book a ticket as soon as possible," And then she went to another room.

Gerald got up sadly and turned to Carol and said: "Damn, they won't leave you alone even here."

"I'm so sorry, but I can't do anything else. That film is a big, expensive project, and everyone involved in it is counting on me. Please try to understand my situation," Carrol replied sadly. "I will be with you again in a few days, I'd better book a ticket there as soon as possible." She made a call to book a ticket for the next day.

At night, when she sent the children to their room, Rose, who was saddened by the news of her mother leaving, said: "I hope the caravan of joy comes here tonight and takes us all to the city of happiness."

Carol kissed Rose's face kindly and said: "No, darling, the caravan of joy will not come here for a few days. The caravan waits for me to come back here and then it will take everyone to the city of joy, only you have to be very careful of that snowman." She kissed the children and left the room.

***

The next day, Roger prepared the car to take Carol to the airport, but Gerald told him that he would take her instead, with the children. He had promised children that after their mother's flight, he would take them to a playground in the city. Gerald got behind the wheel and Carol sat next to him and

children in the back seat of the car and headed for the airport.
The weather was sunny but cold and parts of the road were
frozen. In the middle of the road, a large truck carrying wood
and tree trunks was in front of them. Gerald was waiting for an
opportunity to overtake the truck, but the road was narrow and
other cars were passing by.

The tree trunks were tied with ropes to the back of the truck,
but after a while some of the ropes were loosened and suddenly
several tree trunks fell to the ground from behind the truck.
Seeing the tree trunks moving towards their car, Carol shouted:
"Be careful!"

Immediately her mother's love and instinct made her turn her
head and try to protect her children, but the accident happened
quickly and after colliding with some of the tree trunks, Gerald
lost control of the car, and now it started spinning. Fragments
of past events and memories, like a movie, engulfed Carol's
mind. Memories, and events of many years past and overtook
her body and soul with unimaginable speed.

In her childhood, she had fallen from the top of a tree and
now was spinning and hovering in the air, quickly
approaching the ground. She once appeared in a war movie,

and now the bombs from the planes were falling on her. She was sitting in the Mirror Room and had covered her head with a cloth and was thinking about death and cancer. Oh, the sound of horses' feet could be heard, surely a caravan of joy will pass over our heads. In one of her films, she appeared in the role of the wife of a general and now he was next to a column of slaves and was looking for his wife. A Roman soldier on a chariot drawn by horses beats a slave with a whip hitting his head and back. In another horror film, she plays the role of a bloodthirsty and criminal woman, the only way to destroy her was a bullet in her heart and now one of the heroes of that movie had shot her heart with a gun. She was in the same war movie again and now the bombs were exploding with a terrible sound around her. She was again in her childhood and now after spinning in the air several times, hit the ground with her hands and knees. She was sitting in the Mirror Room when suddenly the mirrors shattered and exploded, and the sharp fragments of them covered her body.

The caravan of joy had carried her husband and children away but had left her on the ground.

She shouted with all her might: "No, wait, I must be with you, too!"

She made a great effort to get into the chariot that the snowman brought. The snowman drove closer, but suddenly turned into a Roman soldier had with a whip in his hand, and the tip of the whip hit one of her eyes, what a terrible pain and panic, the fear of losing her husband and children and her loneliness. Now she was in a terrifying movie where the hero of the movie shot a bullet in her heart.

All those events passed quickly through her mind, and now her body was sending news of her injuries to her brain. Suddenly a dazzling light came over her. Oh, I'm dead, what is this dazzling light? Am I in heaven? She was naked under a waterfall, just like years ago when she went on holiday in a hot country. The water with its magical fluid flowed from her head to the rest of her body and brought a wonderful and unique calmness. Oh, life-giving water, penetrate my eyes and heart. Her mother's loving hands embraced her fallen hands and knees from the tree and embraced her warmly. Her arms longed for her husband and children; she was in a halo of dazzling light.

Even in those circumstances, her gifted and dynamic mind tried to logically understand the fragments of memories and events she had encountered over the years. Her whole soul and body was experiencing death.

***

She had been in a coma for ten days. She was the only one who had survived, her husband and children had died in the accident. Sometime after the accident she was taken to hospital by helicopter. Both of her arms and one leg were broken in several places, she also lost one eye and suffered a heart attack due to her injuries. Her skin and other parts of her body were also injured. The worst skin injury was on her chest and her whole neck up to the chin. For a moment, she heard two women talking, she thought to herself that she had stepped back into her memories, but that was not the case. She could smell the hospital and the various medicines mixed with the scent of flowers. She had a bandage on one of her eyes.

Feeling very lethargic, she opened her other eye, still not knowing where she was or what had happened. There were two nurses talking next to her bed. She stared at the two in surprise for a while and then decided to ask them a question, but her tongue was very heavy, and her lips were numb. She only managed to clear her throat.

As soon as the nurses heard her, they hurried to her and stared at her happily; One of them hurried out of the room to call the doctor, and the other nurse kindly put her hand on Carol's shoulder and said: "Oh my God, how good it is, you have regained consciousness. All your friends and family have told us that you are hardworking and determined and you will not give up and fight for your life."

Carol tried to say something again, but only a few moaning sounds came out of her mouth.

The nurse immediately kindly said: "Calm down, everything is going well, you are now in the hospital, and we will take good care of you." Moments later, several doctors entered the room and carefully performed various tests on Carol, all of whom were happy that she was out of a coma. Carol spent another two days asleep and numb, the pain only occasionally waking her up.

One day she woke up with pain in her eyes and body. She had more strength to speak. Now that she knew that she had been taken to the hospital after an accident, she was more worried about her children and husband than about her own physical condition.

She asked the nurse that day: "Where are my children and husband? Are they injured too?"

The nurse said kindly: "The doctor will see you in a few hours, and you can ask him any questions you have."

Carol, who felt bad about the nurse dodging her question, asked angrily: "I asked you a question, why don't you answer me?"

"I just came to work, and I don't know anything, as I said, the doctor will see you soon."

Sometime later, two doctors, one of whom was a psychologist, visited Carol. One of them was going to explain the injuries to her, but Carol said sadly: "First tell me, what happened to my children and husband?"

Another doctor, a psychologist, approached her kindly and, after giving an introduction and a description of the accident, informed her of the death of her children and husband. Carrol, who had felt for a while that something bad must have happened to her family, was left with only a sad silence, after which another doctor began to describe her injuries and gave her hope that over time, she would regain much of her health. Fractures and injuries to her arms and legs were repairable, and she could have an artificial eye to replace the lost one. After that incident, she had to take great care of her heart. After hearing the news about herself and her family, she closed her eyes again, looking for the same dazzling light. She thought that her children and husband were in the light that symbolized death, but she wanted to return to death or maybe another life, where she could hug her husband and children again, but now she only could feel the pain in her body, and there was no sign of the dazzling light of death.

While she was in the hospital, only her parents were allowed to see her. The news of her accident was spread through the media, but the hospital authorities didn't allow anyone other than her family to visit her, and only once a summary of her condition was announced.

**

Days, weeks, and months passed with deadly weight. Her injuries were healing, and she was walking and doing the exercises she needed every day with different therapists. At first, she refused any exercise or physical therapy for weeks and liked to be in bed most of the time and take painkillers. Her soul was more injured than her body. Finally, after hours of visits a psychologist, at the urging of her parents, had begun to do the exercises.

One day Richard came to see her with a beautiful bouquet, until that day she did not want anyone to see her except her parents, and she refused to see anyone else who came to visit her. She didn't even want to see her friend Gloria. Richard had been to the hospital several times during that time, and each time he was refused entry. Each time he gave flowers to the nurses to take to Carol's room.

For some time, the nurses around her encouraged her to see others, the only visible injuries were an eye and part of her chest and neck. Now she always wore sunglasses and covered her neck with a shawl. Finally, she agreed to see Richard. Richard entered her room with a sad face, trying to smile, and stared at Carol for a moment.

"Why are you wasting your time?" said Carol in a voice of anger and indifference. "What do you want from me?" she took off her glasses and at the same time opened her scarf and said: "Look, these are the wounds of my body, I am sorry that I can't show you the wounds of my soul, those wounds are much more severe and deeper. Don't waste your time on me. I do not need anyone's consolation."

Richard, shocked by Carol's words and deeds, replied calmly: "Nothing has changed in you. You are still the beautiful and lovable Carol."

"It's as if you've lost your ears, I told you I do not need anyone to comfort me." Carol replied in a loud, angry voice.

Richard put the flowers in a vase and sat quietly on a chair by Carol's bed, tears streaming down his cheeks. He had lost the power of speech out of his sheer   sadness.

Seeing Richard's tears, Carol shouted again: "Why are you crying? Who are you crying for? For me? For my children? For my husband? Or for yourself?"

Richard took a handkerchief from his pocket, wiped away his tears, and said: "I'm sorry," and then got up and walked to the front door.

But before he left, Carol said in a firm, decisive voice: "Wait, I want to talk to you."

Richard returned to his chair and stared at the floor as he tried not to look at Carol. After a few moments, Carol said to him: "Hey, Richard, look at me, you'd better get your mind off me, why are you crying? I have never been able to cry myself, you'd better stop feeling sorry for me too."

Richard, who was very upset and tormented, replied softly: "Okay, whatever you say, I am not here to argue with you, I will do whatever you say with pleasure."

"My parents are old," Carrol said after a while. "I would like you to oversee my finances and administration for a while and, most importantly, to deal with journalists, of course, it has been months since the accident, and I hope it has been mostly forgotten. I have agreed to have an artificial eye implanted, and this will probably be done by next week; I will probably be released from the hospital in a few weeks, I don't want to be exposed to the news and public view anymore. I don't need the sympathy of anyone. I just want to be left alone."

Richard nodded his head in agreement and said: "I will do my best, but you know very well that it is difficult, it is still a matter of interest for the public and people are still talking about you."

"But over time, everything will be resolved."

"Yes, over time everything will improve, and you will be able to return to your favourite profession."

Carol frowned and said: "Is that how you want to help me? I told you I never want to go back to acting; I think I was wrong to ask you for help."

Richard kindly responded: "I'm sorry, I'll do whatever you say, I'll do whatever I can. So, it's possible that you'll be released in the next few weeks, huh?"

"Yes."

"Will you do anything about the scars on your neck?"

"These are my wounds, and it has nothing to do with you or anyone else," Carol said angrily. "I will especially keep these wounds so that no one thinks about encouraging me to act again, and I want Sandra and Roger to continue working at my home. I will introduce you to my lawyer and you can take care of my finances."

"Yes, of course, thank you very much for trusting me."

Carol, with a bitter smile, said: "Trust? I don't have much to lose, now I do not have much wealth and opportunities, without my husband and children, the whole world is worthless and useless." Richard was about to say something, but Carol said in a decisive tone: "Enough," and then took a card from her purse and handed it to Richard, saying: "This is my lawyer's number. I have already told him that you would probably accept to oversee my finances. Now please go and leave me alone."

Richard stared at Carol's sad and bitter face for a moment, then left.

***

It had been a few days since she had an artificial eye skilfully implanted, and was quite like her other eye, but she always wore her sunglasses; she was to be released from the hospital in a few days. It was evening when she first spent some time outside in the hospital grounds. She did not know what to do on her own. In the past, whenever she was under work or emotional pressure, she took refuge in acting, and by immersing herself in the roles she had to play, she reduced her discomfort and tension, but now with the great sorrow that filled her soul, she found no refuge.

It was getting dark when she decided to return to her room. When she went up the stairs of the building to go to her room on the second floor, she noticed an exit door on the upper floor which was half open. It was the exit door to the roof of the building; she decided to go to the roof for a while and stare at the sky and the stars. There was a bench on the roof, which was a fairly large area. She sat on the bench and stared at the sky for a long time, after a while she shouted angrily at the sky: "No, you had no right to make me suffer like this, you took everything from me at once, no, you cannot be my God. What did I do? What sin had I committed that you torment me like this? You took everything from me, you took my loved ones and put me in darkness, you made me so lonely and broken. No, you cannot be my God."

She sat on the bench for some time and then approached the edge of the roof and raised her head to the sky again and said: "That wasn't the caravan of joy, it was the caravan of death, you did not even consider me worthy of death, it was the caravan of death, the death of my loved ones, I want to go with them too." After a few moments of silence, she remembered the scene of the accident. She remembered how the car spun, she remembered her childhood when she fell from a tree and hit the ground; she looked down at the hospital grounds. If she had thrown herself down from there, she might have hit the ground only after one or two turns and embraced death. She said to herself, "I have tasted death. I crossed the borders of death in that accident and was thrown back to life. I have experienced that dazzling light and eternal peace of death. I am sure if I spend more time in the world of death, I will find my husband and children again; I am only a few seconds away from that world of light."

Suddenly the voice of the nurse behind her brought her out of her dark world, the nurse asked: "Are you alright?"

"Yes" she replied sadly: "I just wanted to get some fresh air."

"You'd better go back to your room; I have to lock the roof door."

Carol shook her head and went back to her room and went to bed, that night again she had to burn in emptiness without her lost loved ones.

***

After being discharged from the hospital, she asked her driver, Roger, before returning home, to go to the cemetery where her husband and children were buried. Her parents were in the car with her. It was the first time Carol had visited the graves of her husband and children.

Her mother said to her with great sorrow: "My dear, it would be better to wait for a while until you are completely well, you can go to their graves later."

"No, I'm fine," Carol replied sadly but firmly. "We'd better go there today."

When they arrived at the cemetery and Carol found the location of the graves, she turned to the others and said:

"Please leave me for a moment; I'd like to spend some time alone with my loved ones," and then got close to the graves with flowers next to them; she stared at them for a while and felt for a moment that her legs could not bear the weight of her body, she felt a heavy pain in her chest and heart, she sat by the graves and stared at them again, her whole soul was full of sorrow and various memories of her lost loved ones. Memories that did not leave her alone even for a moment after that accident. She could not cry at all, she put her hands on the graves of her children so that she might be able to revive the joy and feeling of touching them. But nothing was waiting for her except the coldness of the tombstone.

She said to herself under her breath: "How easily and suddenly I lost you, I should have been with you."

After a while, her parents and Roger approached her, put her back in the car, and drove home. When Carol entered her house, memories of her husband and children took over her soul deeply. After a few moments she went to her bedroom. Her chest and her whole body were filled with weakness and pain. She lay on her bed and closed her eyes, wishing her heart would stop working and she could let go of this painful sorrow and darkness.

Her parents stayed at her house for several weeks to make sure Carol was getting better and to reduce her loneliness. During those few weeks, Carol was often in her room, just going out to eat and not showing interest in talking about anything.

One day after dinner, she turned to her mother and said:

"Thank you very much for helping me. You can now return to your home. I know you are more comfortable there, I'm fine. And I don't need anyone."

Her mother replied sadly: "Don't worry about us at all, we want to be here. You are still very sad and depressed; we have to be with you longer."

"No, I don't need you," Carol replied sadly. "I would like to be alone for a while now. I must be able to live a new life without my husband and children. As I said, I'm fine. If you want, you can come to see me. Roger and Sandra have worked for me for many years, I will not be alone. Rest assured; I will let you know if I need you." Then she got up from the dining table and went to her room.

Her mother turned to her husband with concern and said: "What should we do? I think she is still very sad and depressed. She should not come back to this house at all, she could go somewhere else, here brings to life the memories of her husband and children."

Her husband shook his head sadly and said: "You know her well. When she decides to do something, no one can stop her. Now she wants us to leave. She wants to be alone. I would not like to leave her alone, but what can we do? All we can do is keep in touch with her. Also, it is better to ask Roger and Sandra to let us know immediately if they find out about any illness or difficulty. No more work can be done by us. When she was in hospital, I asked her several times to sell this house and get a house near us, but she didn't want to, she would like to be in this house.

***

It had been a few days since her parents had left Carol's house, she was now lonelier than ever. She had no patience for anything, she could not read books or listen to music. She spent many hours in her bed, often thinking about her memories. She passed by the door of the Mirror Room several times, but each time she looked with disgust at the closed door. She had no desire for acting or film again.

One day Richard came to see her at home, he called her before he came, but Carol didn't want to see him. Richard had told her that he must come to see her for some financial and administrative matters, and that he had no choice but to visit her.

Richard carried a bouquet of flowers as usual, and when he saw Carol, he smiled and asked: "How are you?"

Carol replied indifferently: "Our relationship is just a legal relationship."

"Yes, I know, I'm not looking for anything else, I am just going to help you," and at the same time he gave Carol some of the papers in the file and said: "Please read them carefully, and if you accept them, sign them."

Carol signed the papers without reading them, saying, "Well, was that all? Now you can go."

Richard stared at Carol for a moment in frustration, then said: "There's something else."

"What?"

"I have been able to avoid talking to journalists about you to a large extent, but all of them are still looking for you. I can no longer keep them away from you with excuses."

"What should I do?" Carol replied sadly. "I can't even bear to see my parents. Tell them that I don't want to be in the news again, now my life is difficult enough, I no longer have the patience to be interviewed by reporters."

"You know better than anyone else that they do not give up so easily, you have been in it for years, and you know very well that you simply cannot get away from everything," Richard said sadly.

"So, what should I do?"

Richard stared at Carol for a moment and said: "I have a good idea. Do you remember Angela from the TV show?"

"Yes, I have been on her show many times."

"I think you should go to that show once again and briefly explain your situation. It is a good opportunity to ask everyone to leave you alone for a while."

"No, I will never appear in front of any camera again."

"So, you want reporters to gather in front of your house and bother you more? You make it worse by not appearing. I know this must be very hard for you, but you will help yourself the most by appearing on TV. Angela is a close friend of mine. I can ask her to give you a list of questions that she wants to ask you beforehand, and you can think about them and give a convincing answer. As I said, you can ask others to leave you alone for a while until you get a full recovery. This is the best thing you can do, otherwise you will encourage reporters and friends to be more curious."

Carol thought for a moment and said sadly: "But I can no longer appear in front of the camera."

Richard replied: "If it is due to your injuries; I can postpone your interview for another time, and you will have enough time to have plastic surgery on your chest and neck. I know one of the best surgeons in this field. You are a very beautiful and attractive woman even with these injuries."

Carol looked violently at Richard and said: "I told you before that these are my wounds, and they have nothing to do with you or anyone else."

Richard stared at Carol for a moment and then said: "It wasn't your fault, why are you punishing yourself? You better listen to the news and radio or television again, thousands upon thousands of people die because of catastrophes such as floods and earthquakes, what is the point for the survivors of those calamities to consider themselves responsible and guilty?"

Carol said bitterly: "Enough, I do not have the patience for your advice," and walked into her room for a while before saying: "Well, you better arrange a short interview. I must be separated from the world of film forever. Send me the questions a few days before the interview, I will have to think about them a bit, you better go now."

Richard sadly looked at Carol's face and shook his head and left.

***

It had been a few days since she had received the questions that she was supposed to answer on the TV show. She remembered the times when she would get a script and prepare for it, but in the past, this was fun and exciting for her, but now, the thought of having to go in front of the camera again bothered her. Although she only had to be on the show for a few minutes, it was very difficult for her to reappear in front of the camera and talk about that accident and her life now. But she knew she had to do it, otherwise she would be constantly harassed by reporters and her fans. She did not know how to be in front of the camera, she hated to wear beautiful clothes and make-up again. On the day she had to go to the studio to be interviewed, several times she tried to enter the Mirror Room to choose the right clothes for that day, but each time she went to the door, she was not able to enter it; Finally, she asked Sandra to go in and bring her a simple and suitable dress. She covered the front of her chest and neck with a scarf and put on sunglasses as usual.

Sometime later, Richard drove her to the studio; Angela, who hosted the show, came to see Carol before the show began and greeted her sadly.

Carol was very upset that she had to go in front of the camera again and said to Angela: "Please do everything briefly, I'm still not completely well."

Angela replied kindly: "Yes, whatever you say, do you want our hairdressers to do some makeup on your face and hair before you start?"

"No, I just want this to end as soon as possible. I do not need any makeup."

"Of course, you are still beautiful and attractive without any makeup."

Minutes later, Carol and Angela sat down at a table, and programmers began adjusting the cameras and lights. Immediately after the light shone on her face, she felt strange, she remembered death and that dazzling light, her heart pounded for a while. Angela kindly put her hand on Carol's hand before the cameras started and said: "Are you okay? Oh, why is your hand so cold? Would you like a hot drink? We are in no hurry."

"No, thank you, just finish as soon as possible."

Moments later the programme began, and now little by little Carol began to feel the calm of death. During the interview, she briefly referred to the accident and thanked her friends and fans for their messages of sympathy, adding that it would take a long time to return to cinema and film and that she might never be able to return.

At the end of the interview, Richard, who had been watching the interview, walked over to Carol, and said: "As always, you are a professional in every sense of the word. You did it with admirable strength and calm."

Carol looked at Richard and said: "It was not my peace and strength; it was the peace and strength of death."

"What? What are you saying?"

"You'd better get me home as soon as possible; I do not have the patience to argue with you."

Richard walked over to the car with her, surprised and worried, without saying a word. On the way, Carol was silent with a serious expression, staring at the distant horizon. Richard tried to talk to her several times, but each time seeing Carol's serious face and strange silence prevented him from doing so. Finally, after a while, he dared to ask: "I wanted to ask you something, I didn't understand the meaning of these words, what do you mean by the peace and power of death?"

Carol stared at Richard for a moment, then said softly: "I experienced death in the accident. I saw the dazzling light of death. When a flash of light shone on my face today, I remembered the accident. I don't know after the accident, how long I have been in a world of light, a world that relieves my pain and gives me a certain peace."

Richard thought for a moment and said: "It's because of the function of the human brain."

"What do you mean?"

"When we humans face big or dangerous accidents, especially if they happen quickly, our brains order the release of chemicals to reduce the pain of injuries and make death easier. I saw a programme some time ago in which several people had a fate like yours, and each of them was involved in dangerous events. Some of them also spoke of light and calm immediately after the accident. A brain surgeon attributed it to the secretion of substances, a chemical in the brain."

Carol shook her head and said: "Whatever it was, it was very strange and powerful. It didn't matter to me whether it was the work of my brain, God or a place in heaven."

Sometime later they reached the front of Carol's house. Carol thanked Richard and got out of the car. Richard got out of the car immediately and said: "Carol, may I see you sometimes?"

"See me for what? If you need my signature for any papers and documents, mail them to me or you can call me."

"No, I wanted to take you out to eat or drink if you want, you must feel lonely in this house, I promise to ask you only as a friend."

"If I need to go out for food or drink, I'll let you know, I don't want to see anyone right now." Carol replied sadly.

"Yes, I understand, please contact me whenever you need something or whatever I can do."

Carrol headed home without answering.

***

While starring in various films, she had become accustomed to thinking about them for a while, even after filming different scenes. By thinking about the previous scenes of the film, she prepared herself better for the next scenes that had not yet been filmed. As usual, she recalled the interview she had had with Angela that day. As she lay in bed, she remembered the moment when the spotlight covered her face and the feeling that she had felt some time later. After the ray of light from the spotlight in her interview, she felt calm, a deadly calm, after remembering that moment, she suddenly got up and went to the Mirror Room, before entering, she said to herself: "Yes, I can experience that peace again in my home and in the Mirror Room."

After entering the Mirror Room, she turned on the room lights and spent some time there. After a few minutes, she left the room and asked Roger to buy some spotlights and install them in the Mirror Room. Roger left the house in surprise, and a few hours later returned home with several spotlights and went to the Mirror Room. During that time, Carol placed a curtain in the Mirror Room with a film projector. When Roger arrived, Carol asked him to place the spotlights in the four corners of the room. It created an atmosphere of dazzling light. Carol then asked Roger to leave the room; After leaving the room, Roger met Sandra in the hallway, who asked him with great enthusiasm and curiosity: "What is she doing there?"

"I don't know, she just asked me to install the spotlights, she herself placed the curtain and the video projector in that room." Sandra happily clasped her hands together and said: "Oh, well then she's getting ready to act in movies again," and then she raised her head to the sky and said: "Oh God, thank you for accepting my prayers."

Carol first locked the door of the Mirror Room and then sat down in her usual chair. The rays of light, in addition to the dazzling brightness, brought warmth to her. She spent some time trying to immerse herself as much as possible in the world of mirrors.

After a while she projected a film that she had previously taken of herself and her children and her husband. Now the images of the children and her husband were not only on the screen but also reflected in various mirrors. For some time, she found herself in the company of her family among the mirrors, when suddenly there was a knock on the door of her room. Sandra was behind the door, asking if she was ready for dinner.

She immediately got up, turned off the film and spotlights, opened the door, and angrily said to Sandra: "When I come to this room, I don't like to be disturbed by anyone." Then she came out and locked the door and said to Sandra: "From now on, I like to participate in household chores, from shopping to cooking and cleaning. I haven't done much physical work and exercise; I have to recover a little."

Although Sandra was shocked by her anxious tone, she smiled when she heard her and said: "Very well, I'm really happy to see you healthier. You really made the right decision to forget about that accident."

"Forgetting? No, I will never forget it."

"Yes, of course, but life goes on and you are a fighter as always."

Carol just shook her head and walked away. She had now managed to escape the harsh world of reality. Now, with her strong imagination, she could laugh, cry and marvel again in the world of film and mirrors. That is why she decided to go back to exercising, paying attention to eating the right foods and participating in the daily routine of life. She knew the world of film better than anyone.

***

Days and weeks passed, and Carol became more and more immersed in the world of film, memories, and mirrors. The bitterness of her reality, loneliness and the accident itself led her more and more to the world of mirrors, a world in which she could keep herself away from the real world. That world also had its own rules and order. There she could not only revive the feeling of being with her lost family, but she could also find and entertain herself with the great love of her life, film and theatre.

Whenever she opened the door to the wardrobe in the Mirror Room and saw the clothes she had previously worn in a movie, she remembered the movie and the story. She remembered how she prepared herself for that film and revived the script and the story in her mind and soul and kept herself busy in this way for hours.

One day, while cleaning the table, Sandra saw Carol leave the Mirror Room in a beautiful dress that must have been from ancient Rome, and approached her with firm steps and a serious, stern face.

Sandra smiled and said: "Oh, what a beautiful dress, I remember well the dress in which you played in the historical film."

At that moment, Roger entered the room and looked at Carol in surprise.

Carol stared at the two with a malicious gaze. Roger asked sadly: "What happened? Are you okay?"

"Curse you, curse you for killing my children and enslaving my husband, my innocent children were just little flower seedlings, flowers that with your hands destroyed, the song of their childish joys has not yet been extinguished in the corners of this desert of madness, you have also enslaved my husband. The light of his sword and the sound of his horse's hooves are still reflected in those mountains. You also imprisoned me in the harem of your lust and depravity. But you have never been able to possess my soul, you have conquered and kicked my body, but you can never chain my soul. Now listen well, can you hear my children's song? Can you hear the footsteps of the horses? Horses, around each of whom sit free men, men who will finally break your tyranny, and now me with a free and militant spirit watching your death and destruction. Come and see your humiliation and smallness in my eyes." After a few moments, Carol returned to the Mirror Room with pride and firm steps.

Surprised, Sandra and Roger stared at each other for a moment, then Sandra happily began to applaud and said out loud:

"Bravo. Bravo, Mrs Carol, you are still a great actress." Roger, who was still quite surprised, asked Sandra if Mrs Carol was playing a role.

"Oh, yes, of course I remember the movie in which she played the same role years ago, she has not lost her acting power yet. I am very happy that she is seriously rehearsing again. She will soon be completely healthy and regain her composure and return to her profession."

Roger, who was still surprised, said: "I was shocked, I couldn't believe that she was playing a role at all, I now really and truly believe that she is one of the best actors."

Hours later, Carol, dressed in her usual clothes, left the Mirror Room, and began to eat as usual. Sandra happily approached her and said: "I am very happy that you are getting healthier and stronger every day. I knew that the passage of time was the greatest cure."

Carol just smiled and said to Sandra at the end of her meal: "I'm going out for a walk," and then left.

***

Another night, Sandra and Roger were sitting at a table in the kitchen drinking. It was a rainy and stormy night, and sometimes the sound of thunder could be heard. For some time, a strange sound of music could be heard from the Mirror Room. The sound of the music mixed with the sound of storms and lightning had created a strange and terrifying atmosphere. Sandra turned to Roger and said: "I've never heard Carol listens to such music so loud, she must be rehearsing for another role." They spent some time at the table talking and drinking.

A moment later, Sandra was about to go to her room when she saw Carol by the kitchen door. Carol, who had made up her face and hair in a strange and frightening way, stared at two of them with a smile. As soon as Sandra saw Carol, she was terrified, and dropped the glass she was holding and stepped back involuntarily. At that moment, Roger noticed Carol; he too got up in shock and stared at her. Carol stared at the two for a moment, then said with a smirk: "I'm so thirsty tonight, your blood belongs to me. Now tell me who wants to be first, huh?"

Roger looked at Sandra in horror. At that moment, Sandra took a deep breath and then smiled and said: "Oh, now I understand what role you are playing. I remember you in that horror movie you starred in, but I have to say that tonight you scared us a lot, my heart was about to explode from fear. I just remember when and where I heard that music. This music that you listened to tonight is the music of that movie, isn't it?"

Carol glared at the two and returned to the Mirror Room.

Roger, who was very scared and completely surprised, turned to Sandra and said: "This is not normal, why did she appear like that? We are not making a movie here."

Sandra smiled and said: "Don't worry, haven't you seen that movie?"

"Which movie?"

"The same horror movie in which she played a role."

"No."

"You have been working for Carol for many years, but you have not seen her films yet?"

"No, I do not have much interest in cinema and film, my job is to protect her."

"I suggest you see them at least once, all her films in which she played a role, what would you do if I weren't here with you tonight? Of course, I was very scared at first, but I soon remembered that movie."

"But she should not play such a role, no one is making a film here and she is not going to appear in a film in the near future."

"Oh, you don't know these actors well, they have a strange world for themselves, especially skilled and powerful actors like Carol."

"I see nothing but madness in Carol's behaviour."

"No, you are wrong, she was hardworking and obsessive in her work from the very beginning. It may seem strange to us as normal people, but she has been practicing hard for some time. I personally prefer to see her active and lively. Do you remember the post-accident period when for a long time she did nothing? I was very worried about her at that time; she was very sad and depressed, but now she is recovering over time. I am sure she will return to the world of cinema soon. Don't worry too much, as I said, you better watch all her films at least once, this way you will be less scared or surprised."

Sometime later, Carol, dressed as usual, came back to the kitchen, and went to the fridge with a smile and poured some milk into a glass, and after drinking it, turned to Roger and Sandra, and kindly said good night to them, and went to her room.

After Carol left, Sandra smiled again at Roger and said: "Did you see? As I told you, she is practising and there is nothing to worry about."

***

One day, Carol saw Sandra sitting in a room watching a movie on TV. Carol stood next to Sandra, watching the movie, and said: "Oh, this is one of the most beautiful love stories."

"Yes, I have seen this film ten times, but each time it is more interesting and beautiful for me than the last time," said Sandra.

"Yes, Casablanca is one of the classic movies, I like it too."

Sandra turned to her and said: "I will never forget the love story movie you starred in, it was a very beautiful and romantic movie."

"Yes, I was very lucky at that time, because it was shortly before that movie that I met my husband and I no longer needed to research and get to know about love and affection, I was totally in love."

Hearing these words, Sandra left the room crying under the pretext of checking the food she was cooking. Carol stared at the television with longing and sadness and remained there until the end of the film.

After the end of the film, she went to the Mirror Room like someone who has missed something so much, hoping that maybe the world of film and mirror would reduce her nostalgia.

The next day, Carol left the Mirror Room for breakfast wearing a beautiful dress and make   up that made her look years younger.

"Oh, what a beautiful dress," Sandra said happily as soon as she saw her.

"Yes, this is one of my favourites," said Carol, who felt young and light-headed.

"Yes, you look very fresh and young today; I am very happy to see your happiness and health."

"Yes, as you said before, life goes on. I now feel young and energetic, we must smile at life with all its hardships," and then she eagerly ate her breakfast. She laughed a lot during breakfast and joked with Sandra.

After a while, like a young girl, she enthusiastically approached the phone and dialled Richard. When Richard picked up the phone, she said enthusiastically: "Hey Richard, how are you?"

Richard, who could not believe at all that Carol had called him, after a moment of silence asked in surprise: "Carol, is that you?"

"Yes, were you waiting for another woman?"

"No, I'm just surprised, how are you?"

"I'm fine, but you still haven't heard my surprise, what are you going to do tonight?"

"I don't have a specific plan, do you?" Richard said in surprise.

"So why don't you and I go somewhere to eat a good meal and listen to music and most importantly dance a little?"

Surprised, Richard paused again and then said happily: "Why not? I can't believe you asked to spend the night with me."

"I haven't made a decision about the whole night yet, I have to see how good you are at your behaviour and then I might decide to spend the whole night with you, but now I don't promise anything," Carol replied with a smile.

"Oh, I cannot believe it, I am very happy with your health and happiness, and I have full confidence in my ability to deal with beautiful and attractive women."

"We'll see about this soon," Carol said with a laugh. "I'll be waiting for you this evening," and then she said goodbye.

All day, until the afternoon, she listened to music and joked with Sandra like a young woman, happily, lightly and mischievously.

In the evening, Richard came to see Carol. He was wearing stylish clothes and had a bouquet of flowers.

Seeing Richard, Carol walked over to him with joy and laughter, kissed his cheek, and happily took the bouquet from him, saying, "Oh, I love these flowers so much," and then looked at Richard's outfit and laughed "You've made a good and professional start today, but it remains to be seen how you will spend the rest of the night."

Richard smiled and said: "Don't worry at all, you have only seen a small part of my skill, I will prove it to you." Then they both went to the car that was parked outside the house.

Before reaching the car, Carol held hands with Richard, as if she saw him as her lover. Richard could not believe that Carol had changed so much. She did not even want to see him after the accident, but now she was behaving like a woman full of joy and love.

Having loved Carol dearly for years, he could not believe his sudden luck at all. He thought he might be dreaming, but no, he was right. Carol was by his side with her beautiful body and soul, and he witnessed her enchanting joy and laughter.

That night they went to a bar and a restaurant where they could dance with each other as well as eat. While eating, Carol's gestures and words, like a clear river full of love and affection, occupied and bathed Richard's soul and mind, and Richard, who, after years of unrequited love, had the opportunity to reach her. He had found something precious and was still in shock. He was drawn in her beauty, tenderness, and talent. Richard had opened his heart completely to the warmth of being in love with Carol. After a while, when the music started playing, he turned to Carol and asked: "Would you like to dance?"

Carol smiled and said: "Yes, I love this song." And then they danced hand in hand together.

After a few moments, Richard put his mouth close to Carol's ear and said softly: "You have no idea how happy I feel tonight. I did not think I would spend such moments with you even in my dreams. I'm so glad you got over it."

Carol suddenly pulled her hand out of Richard's and put her finger on Richard's mouth and said: "Be quiet, I don't want to hear anything about the accident."

Richard immediately replied: "Okay, I'm sorry." after a few moments Carol embraced Richard as they danced.

Now she could feel the warmth of Richard and even hear his heartbeat. After a few moments, she took off her sunglasses and looked into Richard's eyes, which were staring at her lovingly, and said: "This is me, all of me, do you still want to love me?"

"Yes, you know better than anyone else that I have loved you for years, but I have not yet understood all of you, and even you yourself still don't know how talented you are   " replied

Richard, with tears in his eyes. "I, nor even you, do not fully understand the beauty of your creative soul and mind, a creativity that makes us laugh and cry and that can burn."

Carol, who felt a strange love and beauty in Richard's beautiful words, put her head back on Richard's chest and after a while softly whispered a poem in Richard's ear:

The ice melts

In my Soul

In my thoughts

Spring

Is your presence

Being you (1)

Richard, who was overwhelmed with excitement and love when he heard the poem, hugged Carol tightly and said: "Let's start a new life together," and then they danced in silence for some time.

That night Carol went to Richard's house, and they passionately made love. Early in the morning, Carol got out of bed and stared at Richard's sleeping face for a while. After putting on her clothes, she picked a flower stem from the vase and placed it next to Richard and left.

When she got back to her house, she went immediately to the Mirror Room.

A few hours later she came to the table to eat. Sandra approached her with a meaningful smile and said: "Mr Richard has called several times. I told him you were busy and did not have a chance to talk to him. I didn't want to bother you when you were in that room."

"What else does he want?" Carol replied angrily.

"Nothing, he just wanted to talk to you, he sounded very happy," said Sandra, who was taken aback by Carol's angry tone.

"I told him before that he would only call me when something urgent or important happened, I don't know what he wants from me," Carol said angrily again.

Sandra said in surprise: "I'm sorry, maybe this does not concern me, did you have a fight or quarrel with him last night?"

"You are right, this is none of your business, from now on whenever Richard calls here tell him that I do not want to see him or talk to him, whenever it is necessary to see him, I will call him myself."

Richard tried to contact Carol for several days but was unsuccessful, so he decided to turn up at her house without warning.

As usual, he bought a bouquet and went to Carol's house.

"I'm sorry, Mr Richard, she doesn't want to see you." Sandra said sadly after opening the door.

"Why? Is she okay?"

"Yes, she is OK and is in her room right now, I'm sorry I have to ask you to leave."

"No, I'm not leaving until I talk to her, I'm going to her room now."

Sandra stood in front of him sadly and said: "No, please do not go to that room, she strongly asked us not to allow anyone to enter that room, please wait here, she will come out to eat or drink later. Please also tell her that I asked you to leave but you insisted on seeing her."

Richard shook his head and said: "Well, I'll wait here."

After a while, Carol left the Mirror Room and saw Richard in another room. Richard stared at Carol's face for a while and then went closer to her and asked: "What happened? Why don't you want to see me? Have I done something wrong?"

"I told you before that you should not waste your time on me," Carol said in a serious, dry tone.

Richard said with great surprise: "What are you saying? You seem to have forgotten what a good night we had together."

"No, I still remember, but it belongs to the past, it would be better if you forgot it."

"Forgot it? What are you saying? We both agreed to start a new life together, we both admitted that we love each other."

Carol smiled bitterly and said: "How do you expect me to love you? No, I have never loved you and I will not, do not deceive yourself."

"But you told me you love me, did you forget?" Said Richard, shocked by Carol.

"Oh, it must have been the effect of wine and alcohol, but now I am totally in my right mind, and I tell you again that no, I do not love you."

"You have no right to treat me and yourself like this, you have no right to play with my feelings. What happened to all the warmth and intimacy you showed that night? What happened to all those beautiful and delicate feelings?" As he continued, his eyes filled with tears, and he said: "Why have you now become an iceberg?"

"Are you crying again?" said Carol, still staring indifferently at Richard. "I have never liked weak men," and then she looked at the bouquet that Richard had with him and said: "When you get out of here, take these flowers with you, I do not need them, take your romantic feelings somewhere else too."

"Why are you so cruel?"

Carol stared at him angrily and said: "Cruel? You still don't know the meaning of cruelty, look at me and my life, who has had mercy on me in this life? Look how cruelly I lost everything. No, you still don't know the meaning of cruelty."

Richard, who still could not believe that Carol had mocked him like this, stared at her for a while and then said: "I knew from the first day I saw you that you are a powerful actor, and you can play any role well. I'm leaving here today, and I will never come back, just answer one of my questions, were you the one who spent the night together or did you just act?" Then he nodded and said: "No, it was you, all that love, and intimacy cannot be the only result of someone's acting, that love, and warmth was real."

Carol nodded and said: "Maybe it was real for you, but not for me. It was just another role for me."

Then she turned her back on Richard and left the room.

***

It was evening when she decided to leave the house for a walk. Before leaving the house, Roger reached out to her and said: "Are you going out?"

"Yes, why?"

After a pause, Roger said: "I still don't think it is advisable for you to leave home alone and travel around the city. Let me come with you."

Carol smiled and said: "No, don't worry about me at all. I'm out of the spotlight. I'm history now. No one is looking for me."

"But I feel I have to do something in this house, my main job is to protect you and this house, otherwise I feel that you don't need me."

"As I said, do not worry about me at all, and I'd still like you to be in the house. Don't think that you are not needed, the protection of this house is a big job." Then she left.

She walked through the streets for a while, remembering when she and her husband walked in the city at the beginning of their acquaintance and for a long time, they walked in different parts of the city every day.

She was passing by a building when she saw a sign with the Writers' Association engraved on it. She remembered her husband, who was a writer and had been to such associations many times. She remembered the movie in which she played the role of a writer. Immersed in her memories, she returned home and went to the Mirror Room.

The next evening, she left the house again and went to the same building, part of which belonged to the Writers' Association, and went into an office where a young man was sitting at a desk.

The young man asked cheerfully: "Can I help you?"

"Years ago, I used to sometimes go to writers' groups in different places and attend their storytelling and poetry sessions," Carrol said with a smile.

"Are you a writer yourself?"

"Yes, of course I am not a famous writer and I have written only a few stories and poems so far."

"Very well, we will be very happy for you to attend our meetings Tomorrow night we have a meeting where some young and novice writers will read their work to the people present at the meeting. If you like, I can also give you time and you can read one of your works to us. This is the best way to get to know other people."

"Oh, that's great, it's going to be very exciting for me," Carol replied happily.

The young man said with a smile: "You should not worry at all; We have been able to gather a small group of talented people here. The meeting will start tomorrow night in the small hall in this building. I will personally introduce you to the group and you can also participate and read your writings."

Carol introduced herself to the man by another name and said goodbye to him happily and excitedly, promising to read part of one of her writings tomorrow night. Then she left and returned to her house and went to the Mirror Room.

The next night, she entered the Writers' Association wearing a simple and beautiful dress carrying a notebook. The same man she had met the day before led her into the hall. About 20 to 30 people were sitting in chairs, and in front of them was a small table with several microphones. The man asked her to sit on a chair next to that table. A woman and another man, probably writers, were sitting at the table. The man turned to Carol before introducing her and said: "Are you ready to be the first to read your writing to us?"

"Yes, it doesn't matter to me if I am the first or the last person," Carrol smiled confidently.

The man also smiled and said: "You must be one of the most experienced and professional writers, because I do not see any sign of anxiety or excitement in you, you must have done this, many times."

"Yes, I lived in another city, and we had similar meetings every week, and now it is easy and pleasant for me to read my stories and writings in front of a group."

The man leaned his head a little closer to Carol's ear and said: "I'm still embarrassed when I stand in front of a crowd to speak for them, but you, like a professional and experienced actor, have a high level of confidence in yourself. I'll introduce you to the group now."

After a few moments, he turned to the crowd and asked them to be quiet, and then introduced Carol and said: "We have a new guest tonight, and it would be better if she was the first to read a piece of her writing to us." Then he turned to Carol and said: "Come on, you'd better start."

First, Carol smiled with great power and mastery and then said: "I have just written this piece and it may need more changes and corrections, but in any case, it is a piece that I wrote from the bottom of my heart and with all of my being. I hope that the quotation that says, 'whatever emanates from the heart rests in the heart' is true of my writing and that you enjoy it too." Then she opened her notebook and, after a pause, began to read in a gentle and sad voice:

"We were on a mysterious path and in search of happiness, alas, I didn't know that the earth was thirsty, in the cold and white season, we had only our warm and hopeful hands and souls, in that snow and cold, only the laughter   and joy of my children brought us warmth, we were on a journey to happiness, alas I did not know the earth is thirsty. My husband, as always, was full of love and patience, I had found the greatness of love and life in his hands and eyes for the first time, with the magic caravan of love carried by a powerful and loving horse, towards life and hope and we were eager to move. Unfortunately I didn't know that the earth is thirsty, it is thirsty for the blood of my loved ones. As we passed over the mountains, I saw broken flower stems, but I did not realize that it was the messenger of a catastrophic event. We were looking for life when we were trapped in death.

"I shared my death with the seasons

With the season that was passing

I shared my death with the snow and

With the snow that sat

With birds and

With every bird in the snow

That was in search of a seed

With water stream and

With silence fishes (2)

"It is a pity that I didn't know that the earth is thirsty, thirsty for the blood of my loved ones, I wish I could give my blood to the thirsty earth and satisfy it so that it does not need other blood, but it is a pity that the earth is thirsty, it is satisfied only by the blood of my loved ones. The looting hands of the devil and the accident snatched my loved ones from me and left me alone in the cold and frozen season."

At the same time, tears were falling down her face from under her sunglasses. After a while, she paused and read again:

"And now I'm left to travel through the cold season.

Dew and leaves are frozen

My wishes too

Snow clouds are rolling in the sky

The wind blows and

The storm is coming

My Wounds

Depress (3)

"It was not long after the accident that I got up in search of the sun's heat with a wounded soul and spirit. I asked for help from the mirrors, the mirrors that reflect heat to my tired and wounded body and soul. Mirrors in which I was able to find my loved ones again.

"I come back to life in the light and in the mirrors and I laugh, and I make others laugh, I cry and make others cry, I wonder and make others wonder. It is only in the light and mirrors and memories of my past that I come to life. It is there that I find the smile of flowers, the tears of joy and the bitterness of farewell and death.

"I have mixed my life and existence with the light and fragility of mirrors and I fly lightly in the images suspended in the mirrors, I have found life again in the mirrors, my dreams and loves are wandering in the light and the mirror. I connect the images of my memory and dream with the truth, the truth that may itself be a reflection of the images of the mirrors, yes, I live in the light of the mirror.

"It is only in the world of light and mirrors that I can feel again the glory of life and the greatness of catastrophe and tragedy with all my flesh and blood and bones, it is only in that world that the doves of my hopes spread their wings and take me deeper. The depths of joy, the depths of sorrow and pain.

"Now I can reappear with a joyful spirit and smile, I can feel the colours with their glorious and astonishing beauty, I can see the true colour of suffering and blood, and with the wonderful symphony of life and death, I can now find myself again. I can drown in the music of birds; I can cover myself with blossoms and despair and play love with the most loving men and get lost in the calming running of the water.

"My world is a world of tenderness and steel and fragility, only in this world I can enter the awe of God and the devil, be imprisoned, be a prison guard, sow seeds on the ground or shed blood with a sword, go to the heights of the heavens and or to be buried at the bottom of the living earth, yes, my world carries the world of light and mirrors and darkness in itself, my world is the world of acting and image.

"Thank you."

She performed the piece with such strong and beautiful feeling that it made several people in the audience cry.

Carol quickly wiped away her tears and got up to leave, but the same man who had introduced her to the others said: "Please stay here for a while, you are a newcomer, and read a very beautiful piece, we all want to know more about you, I think a lot of people would like to ask you questions."

Carol nodded sadly and said: "No, I'm sorry, I have to go. I will definitely attend your next meeting and answer your questions." Then she left quickly and returned home.

After that experience, it was only in her own world that she could laugh, cry, rejoice, grieve, be depressed and find a reason to continue living. Her hopes and aspirations were now formed and realized only in the world of mirrors and images.

***

It was a cold autumn day in the evening when she decided to leave the house and take a walk in the city. As she was walking, lost in thought, she found herself in a neighbourhood where prostitutes were standing under streetlights. As she passed some of them, all in revealing clothes and thick make up, one of them mockingly said to her: "Hey babe, are you a newcomer? You'd better clear off from this place and go somewhere else, this place belongs to me and my friends, do you understand?"

"I'm sorry, I just wanted to cross here," Carrol nodded politely, and quickly left.

As she walked back to her house, she remembered a movie in which she played a prostitute. Before starring in the film, she spent some time researching how prostitutes live and work. It was in these thoughts and memories that she entered her house and went to the Mirror Room as usual.

The next night, wearing thick make up and a short skirt, she went to Roger's room and asked him to go out and check the car.

"There is nothing wrong with your car," said Roger, who was surprised to see Carol's clothes and makeup. "I check it every day, I checked it this morning and left it on for a while."

"Better check it again, I want to ride for a little while, I don't want anything wrong with the car."

"Okay, I will check the car again now."

"Well, I'll wait here."

After Roger left the house, Carol hurried into his room, took his handgun from one of the desk drawers in his room, hid it in her handbag, and hurried out of the room. After a few moments, Roger returned home and handed the car keys to Carol, saying, "As I said, there is nothing wrong with your car."

Carol took the car keys. After saying thank you and goodbye to Roger, she left the house and went to her car and drove towards the city. After a while, she parked her car next to a club.

It was a strip club and some women danced naked in front of customers. At the entrance, a bouncer stopped her and said:

"This club will open in another hour, now it is early."

"But I came here to find work and I have to see the boss."

The strong man looked at her with a lustful smile and said: "Come with me," and then they both entered the room where the other two men were sitting at the table and drinking.

The bouncer turned to another man who was supposed to be the boss of the club and said: "This lady has come here to get a job."

The boss looked at Carol with a smile and said: "Oh what a beautiful lady. We don't need a maid or waiter here, only if you want to dance, we can give you a chance. You are a beautiful lady, and you can have a good income."

"Yes, I came here to dance too."

The boss clapped his hands with happiness and said: "Well, we'd better see your artistic show once," and then he turned to the bouncer and said: "Take her to the girls' changing room to get ready," and then winked at Carol and said: "Please, we are looking forward to see your performance."

Carol went to the changing room with the bouncer and changed into another sexy dress. She returned to the hall and got on the stage. Carol first asked the person in charge of playing the music to play her favourite song, and then danced with soft, beautiful movements. As she danced the striptease, she showed her skill. The boss and the other men each watched her with great lust and enthusiasm. When Carol finished dancing and quickly put on some of her clothes and asked the boss: "What do you think? Did you like my dance?"

"Yes, you are one of those professionals, now you have to work for us, I will not lose you easily," said the boss, who had never seen anyone dance with such beauty and elegancy before, and then he got closer to Carol and put his hand on her scarf and said: "Only you should get rid of this scarf and these dark glasses."

Annoyed, Carol pulled back nervously and said: "These glasses and scarf are part of my dance performance."

The boss, who was surprised to see Carol's sudden movement, approached her again with suspicion, and quickly untied her scarf from her neck. After seeing the scars, he frowned and said: "Hey, what are these? With these scars, you only make my clients run away, now take off your glasses."

"I do not want to work here, but I will eventually find your criminal friend and kill him." Carol said nervously as she walked away from them.

The boss asked in surprise: "Who? Which friend?"

"You'd better go and deceive someone else; you know who I am looking for, I am looking for Alex, that friend of yours."

"Alex? Who is he? I don't have a friend with that name," he shouted angrily: "Get out of here, it is not only your chest and neck that are injured, but your brain is also damaged, piss off."

"It's not over yet, I'll find Alex anyway, I promise, and then he will be finished," Carol said with a violent look as she walked out.

Inside herself, she felt humiliated that she had danced naked in front of them, and disgust at the humiliation over her wounds. A mad rage pervaded her being.

When she got home, she said to Roger: "I think you should check the car again. I think there is a fault in its engine."

Roger said in surprise: "I checked it before you left, I didn't find anything wrong."

"Why did I hear unusual noises from the car engine while I was driving? You'd better look at it again now."

"Okay, I'll check it again right now."

When Roger left the house, Carol went back to his room and put the gun in the desk drawer, but due to the rush and the thoughts that filled her mind and soul, she did not put the gun in the right drawer. Instead, she mistakenly put it in another drawer and left the room immediately.

After a while, Roger returned home and said: "The car works fine, but if you want, I can take it to a mechanic tomorrow to make sure."

"No, I need the car again tomorrow. Just before I leave, I'll ask you to check it again." Then she went back to the Mirror Room.

As usual, Roger returned to his room at night after checking the cameras and the corner of the building and locking the doors. As usual he intended to take the gun out of his drawer and put it next to him, but when opened the drawer the gun wasn't there. Surprised and upset, he began to search and after a few moments found the gun in another drawer. He could hardly believe this, he was always very careful where he kept his gun and he knew at every moment where the gun was, but now its location had changed. He was convinced that someone else must have moved the weapon. Again, with great uneasiness and surprise, he looked around the corner and even outside the building for anything suspicious, but everything was normal. No one came in or out of the house except Sandra and Carol.

After a few hours of complete confusion, he went to Sandra and woke her up and said: "Something important has happened and I have to talk to you."

Sandra, who had just woken up, replied angrily: "Can't you tell me about this important event tomorrow morning?"

"No, this is very important."

"Tell me what happened."

"I found out today that someone moved my gun from its permanent place to another place. I always put my gun in a drawer of my desk in the room, but tonight I found it in another drawer."

"Maybe you put it in another drawer by mistake."

"No, that is not possible, I have been a security guard for many years, and I would never make such a mistake."

"Now that you have found your weapon, what are you worried about?"

"Don't you realize the importance of this issue? Who moved my weapon? Maybe this gun was taken somewhere for a few hours. This is very important. Tonight, I have checked the camera videos several times, except for you and Carol, no one else has entered or left this house, I am sure this was not your work."

"Do you think Carol did this?" Sandra said in surprise.

"Yes, you should have seen her today, she was wearing thick make-up and sexy clothes and when she returned home, she was very upset and nervous."

"Thick makeup and sexy clothes are not a reason for her to carry a gun."

Roger stared at Sandra for a moment and then said: "Contrary to what you think, Carol is not in a good mood. You attribute her strange behaviour to her rehearsals for different roles, but I don't think it is normal. Today, under various pretexts, she asked me to leave my room and check her car. She had enough time then to take my gun and later put it back in the room, but she accidentally put the gun in another drawer. I'm more worried about her health than anything else. I don't know what to do. I have asked many times if I could accompany her when she wants to leave the house, but she does not allow me to do so."

Sandra, who was now worried, replied: "What should we do now? Maybe it's better to call Richard."

"Do you remember the way she treated Richard?" Roger shook his head sadly. "That's why I think she's not in good mental health. She spends hours every day in that room, what does she do there? You say she is practicing, practicing for what? Does she want to go back to acting again? She herself has said many times that she will never return to acting and the cinema, so what is rehearsal for? I think the issue is more serious than that."

"What should we do now?"

Roger thought for a moment and said: "First we have to make sure it was her who moved the gun."

"How?"

"She told me that she needs the car again tomorrow night, I will put my gun in that desk drawer again, of course, I will take out its bullets, so we can be sure that she is the one who took the gun or not."

***

At night, Carol went to Roger again in the same thick make up and revealing dress and asked him to check the car again before she left. She went to his room again after Roger left and picked up his gun and put it in her handbag and left the house quickly.

Roger had just started the car when Carol told him: "I don't think there is anything wrong with the car. I have to go now." Then she quickly got behind the wheel of the car and left the house.

That night she was going to find a pimp, Alex, by watching the prostitutes on the street. Alex was a fictional character in a movie that Carol had appeared in many years ago. In that movie, Alex was a pimp and killed her friend who was a prostitute. In that film, Carrol had approached Alex's gang and took revenge on her friend.

As she approached the street where the prostitutes were gathering, she parked the car on a corner and watched several prostitutes through the car window. She knew Alex would eventually come to check on the prostitutes. She continued to watch the place and the prostitutes for hours, until finally a car stopped there, and a man dressed very nicely, smoking a cigarette, got out of the car, and joked with some prostitutes. Carol knew that the man must be one of the pimps. She quickly got out of her car, approached the man, pointed her gun at him, and asked in a loud, agitated voice, "Where is Alex?" The man, who was very frightened, answered with difficulty: "Oh, please do not point that gun at me."

"Tell me where Alex is," Carol shouted angrily again.

"Alex? I don't know anyone by that name, please do not hurt me."

"You bastards are very good at protecting your criminal friends, now if you don't say where Alex is, I will put a bullet in your dirty brain."

The man, who was now crying with fear, groaned: "Please don't do anything to me, I don't know anyone by the name of Alex, I swear I do not know such a person, but I can tell you I will help you find him, I promise I will help you do this. I have many friends and connections, I will definitely find Alex for you through them, please don't do anything to me."

Carol stared at the crying face of the man with hatred and said: "I will find him myself, now take off your clothes, now it is the turn of filth like you to entertain us a little."

The man said in surprise: "What?"

Carol shouted angrily again: "Do not waste my time, take off your clothes or I will shoot a bullet in your tearful eyes, hurry up."

The man hurriedly took off his clothes and stood naked in front of Carol. The prostitutes were all staring at the scene in fear. Carol stared at him with contempt for a moment and then shouted, "Run now, you'd better start running as fast as you can."

The man started running in fear, waiting for a bullet to be fired at him at any moment.

Carol quickly got back in her car and drove home. When she entered the house, Richard, along with Sandra and Roger, was waiting nervously for her.

Richard asked anxiously: "Are you okay? Where did you go?"

Carol looked at Richard and said angrily: "What are you doing here? I told you I would call you whenever I needed to." Then she turned to Roger and said: "Ask Mr Richard to leave."

Roger just lowered his head and made no move.

"Hey, are you still working for me?" Carol shouted angrily. "I told you to ask Richard to leave, do you not understand?"

Richard approached her with great sadness and said softly: "We are all worried about you."

"Worried about me? Why?"

Richard paused and then said: "Why are you carrying a gun?"

Carol, who did not expect such a question, replied: "Which weapon? What are you talking about?"

"We know you have Roger's weapon with you. You took that weapon with you yesterday too," Richard said softly. Carol turned to Roger angrily and said: "What right do you have to slander me?"

Roger stared at the ground and replied: "I'm sorry. I found out yesterday that my gun had been moved. I told Sandra about it. Today, I was almost certain that it was you who took my gun. If you want, you can try it, I have taken out all the bullets and the gun is empty."

Carol, who added to her anger at every moment; shouted, "This house and everything in it belongs to me. It's not up to you what I do."

"We're all worried about you," Richard said sadly again.

"Why?"

"Roger and Sandra have told me that you are rehearsing and acting in different roles every day, roles that you have previously played in different movies."

Carol looked at Roger and Sandra angrily and said: "So you are spying on me? You're both fired, pack up and get out of my house as soon as possible." Then she turned to Richard and said: "You'd better leave this house as soon as possible."

"As I said before, we're worried about you, I went to your room, those spotlights and movies and mirrors, what are you doing there?" Richard said in a more forceful tone. "Every day you spend hours of your time there, I remember you well in the way you dress and put on makeup today, you are now in the role of a prostitute who decides to take revenge on a pimp, I remember that movie very well, that's why you stole Roger's gun, that's why we are worried about you, you live in the world of your past memories and movies."

Carol ran angrily to the Mirror Room and when she reached the door, she noticed that it was broken. Concerned and anxious, she entered the Mirror Room, but there was no trace of spotlights or video players in it. Now there were only mirrors in that room. She looked in the mirrors, but there was nothing in them but her own picture, so where did the pictures of the children and her husband go? What happened to that warm white light? For a while she put her hands on the mirrors as if she wanted to go into the world of mirrors, but now she only felt the coldness of the mirrors. "So, I lost my husband and children again in the world of light and mirrors."

At that moment, Richard came into the room and said softly and kindly: "Carol, you better leave this room and this house."

"What happened to my spotlights and movies?" Carol asked angrily. "Who allowed you to invade my privacy?"

"Carol, we all care about you, we love you, you have created an unreal world for yourself here," Richard replied, tears welling up in his eyes.

Carol cried out angrily: "Whatever it was, it was my world, and it has nothing to do with you, you stole my world from me, I was happy in that world, I lived, I shed tears and I rejoiced, you had no right to ruin my world." At the same time, she felt severe pain in her heart and chest, which made her short of breath and she sank to her knees. Richard noticed that Carol was in a bad state, he quickly approached her, Carol's face turned red from her shortness of breath; Richard immediately laid her on the floor and shouted at Roger and Sandra to call an ambulance as soon as possible, as he tried to give first aid to Carol.

***

She was hospitalized for three weeks. After the first week, when most of the medical care was for her heart, a psychologist came to see her regularly. Carol had agreed to take psychiatric medication as well. She fell asleep day and night for a long time while taking those drugs. After several weeks of meeting with a psychologist and taking medications she had just realized what a horrible abyss she had entered. She, who always had a sense of humanity and helping others, and who had never intentionally or knowingly harmed anyone or even an animal, now realized that she had carried a weapon that could have caused death or injured others. She was very scared and anxious and knew that if something like that happened again, she would never be able to forgive herself. That is why she accepted that she had to improve her mental state, because she was afraid that by losing control of her nerves, she would commit an act that would harm others. Although she was getting closer to the real world every day due to rest and the use of medications, the real world was still empty and worthless to her.

One day she stared out the window of her room. Winter had begun and it was snowing. The hospital grounds were covered with snow. Her room was on the tenth floor, and as she looked out the window she thought to herself how good it would be if she could experience that sudden death again for just a few moments, the same death where she had seen her loved ones, perhaps this time she would join them, if only for a short time, like the short time she had in the accident, when their car twisted and flew to their death.

She thought to herself that by jumping out of that window, she would certainly be able to find her family members again and be with them forever. But what if she failed to see them again?

They are dead and death is the end of everything. There was no guarantee that she would be with them even after death, who has ever returned from death? These thoughts had created doubt in her soul and spirit, and the doubt that she might not be able to see her loved ones, even after her death, made life in the real world even more bitter for her.

She thought to herself: I will no longer be able to fall in love with anyone or anything. So, what joy and excitement do I have to be and continue living? The thought that even death would not make her happy was very heavy and painful for her. Time, maybe the passage of time would give her another chance, an opportunity to be able to enjoy love and life again.

***

While she was in the hospital, her parents and Richard visited her regularly. One day Richard, who had brought her a bouquet as usual, told her: "You will be released from the hospital soon. Your parents, the doctors and I think you should not go back to your home, there are so many memories out there that make you sad. I can sell your house and get another one for you near your parents, or you can go to another house you have in another city if you want. After a few moments, he paused and then said: "I have a big house in this city which consists of two separate buildings, I can gladly give you one of those buildings. You can live there for a while and then make your own decision about what you want to do. I can ask Roger and Sandra to continue working for you, that's better; I also promise never to disturb you, this way you won't be alone for a while."

Carol looked kindly at Richard and said: "You have helped me a lot so far. I really apologize for the past. I did not mean to upset you in any way."

"I know, don't even think about it, the most important thing is your health, what do you think now? What should I do? You definitely can't go back to your home."

After a moment of silence, Carol said sadly: "Very well, I'm moving to one of your buildings. The thought that I might re-enter the world of madness scares me so much; I have never deliberately intended to cause trouble for others, now that I think about the path I have taken and the possibility that I might cause the death of others, it is very frightening for me."

"No, you shouldn't blame yourself, this can happen to anyone. I am very happy that you have now decided to take care of yourself, and I and others will do our best to help you."

***

She had been staying at Richard's house for a few months now. Spring, with its charming beauty, could be seen everywhere. Because Richard was so fond of flowers and plants, the whole area of his house was covered with flowers, and inside the rooms of the house there were various beautiful flowers and plants. Whenever he had the chance, took care of the house flowers and plants, otherwise he hired a gardener to take care of them.

But the spring and the flowers, for all their beauty, had little effect on Carol's soul and mind, as if an aura of cloud and dust had enveloped her fascinated and creative soul, keeping her still in the cold and grey season.

One day while she was walking in the yard, Richard approached her and said kindly: "Do you see what a glorious beauty spring has brought with it?"

"Yes, spring has come again, but for me the different seasons are not so different, I just have to wait impatiently for them to come and end," Carol replied indifferently.

Richard said in surprise: "No, I know you well, I know that you love nature and the change of seasons, you yourself told me many years ago that this is a source of inspiration for you."

"Yes, I told you that many years ago, but now the situation is different."

Richard stared at Carol for a moment with sadness and then said, "I'm going on a trip today. I told you before that I was working on a project. Now I have to go to another country for a few months."

Carol was initially envious of Richard for a moment, knowing very well that if life had been normal for her, she would be involved in a project or a movie, but she immediately cursed herself, no, now the world of film brings me nothing but madness; She just shook her head and wished him success and headed for the park near the house.

She walked in the park for a while and then sat on a bench. The noise of families coming to the park with their children and playing games could be heard in the distance. How she wished that her children were with her at that time and that they could play and walk like other children. As she sat on the bench, meditating, she suddenly noticed a man staring at her intently. After a few moments she turned her face to the other side so that she might escape the man's gaze, but the man was still staring at her in surprise, and finally after a few moments he approached her and with a voice that was full of excitement said: "Please forgive me. I recognise you, are you a famous actor?" And he went on immediately and said: "I don't believe this, yes, it is you, can I talk to you for a moment? Please forgive me, I'm so excited, please let me talk to you for a moment."

Carol was not only a good actress herself, but also, with years of experience, well able to recognize the moods and movements of different people. She knew full well that the man was sincerely happy and excited to see her. She smiled and said: "You must be very interested in movies that you recognized me with these sunglasses."

The man said happily again: "Yes, of course you have always been one of my favourite actors and I am very sorry for what happened to you. I think that the world of art and cinema lost one of its best and most valuable people." Then he continued in embarrassment and said: "I mean cinema has lost you temporarily."

At that moment, Roger approached the two and said to Carol: "Are you alright?"

Carol, surprised by Roger's sudden arrival, smiled, and said: "So you're always watching me, huh?"

Roger shook his head, staring intently at the man, and said: "This is my job."

"It doesn't matter, this gentleman is one of my former art lovers, we wanted to talk a little bit, there's no problem, you can go," said Carol, noticing Roger's looks at the man.

Roger shook his head and walked away.

The man asked Carol hesitantly: "Can I sit on this bench with you?"

"Yes, sure."

"This is not really the first time I've seen you up close," the man said after sitting next to Carol.

"Oh, where else did you see me?"

The man said happily: "I am a writer, I saw you one night in the Writers' Association, that night you read a piece of your writing to us. Although you introduced yourself under another name, I guessed from your tone of voice and your skill in performing that piece that you must be my favourite actress. I wanted to have a chance to talk to you in that meeting, but you left the meeting immediately after reading. I must say that in addition to your acting skills, you are also a talented writer. Did you write that piece yourself?"

"Yes, but I do not consider myself a writer, although I also write occasionally. My late husband was a good writer," Carol said with a smile.

The man lowered his head sadly and said: "I am very sorry about the accident; you must have gone through very difficult times."

"You don't intend to talk to me about that incident?"

"Oh, no, my name is Mendoza, I'm from Mexico, but I've been living here for years."

"Yes, I guessed you must have come here from another country."

"You may not believe it," Mendoza said after a moment of silence. "I was writing a story some time before that accident happened to you, and since I am so interested in film and cinema, my characters and the events in it are always subconsciously imprinted in my mind like a movie. There is a female character in that story that is based on you. After that incident happened to you, my story ended more or less like your real life. I have not been able to publish that story yet, but I can give you a copy if you want."

"Yes, of course, why not?" said Carol, who felt good about Mendoza.

Mendoza stood up happily and said: "How can I give you the story?"

"Bring it here tomorrow," Carol said with a laugh.

Mendoza happily shook Carol's hand and said: "Yes, I will definitely bring you a copy of my story tomorrow." Then he walked happily away.

***

Carol spent the whole day and night again thinking about stories, films, and memories. On the one hand, Richard's project and on the other hand, meeting Mendoza had aroused in her the temptation of the story and the film, but at the same time, it had brought her fear and panic. Fear and hesitation that she would go crazy again by concentrating her thoughts on acting. She still didn't know whether it was her fascinated and creative soul that was revived or the world of delusion and madness.

The next day, before going to the park again and seeing Mendoza, without realizing it, her make-up and hair style were just like they were when she first met her husband. Just moments before she left, when she was looking in the mirror, she suddenly came to her senses and immediately undid her hair and cursed herself, saying: "I have been led back to my memories from the very first moment. No, I should no longer deceive myself or others, I cannot go crazy, no, I should never think of another story or movie again."

After a while, she left home sadly and went to the park. Mendoza had been waiting for her there for some time. Seeing her, he approached her happily and said: "Oh, you don't know how happy I am. This is a copy of my story." After taking the story, Carol thanked him in a dry but polite tone and said goodbye.

"My address and phone number are on the bottom page, please tell me your opinion about the story. It is important to me," Mendoza told Carol before leaving.

Carol just nodded and said goodbye. When she returned home, she put the story on a table in her room and said to herself: "No, I will never read a story again, especially one that is similar to my own."

***

It had been a week since she had taken that story from Mendoza, but she had not read a word of it, but from the first moment the temptation to read that story had taken over her soul and being. Again, like when she got a good script, her whole mind was fixed on reading it carefully to understand the story in depth, but now, apart from the grief and dust of despair that had filled her heart and soul, there was the fear of stepping back to temptation of movies and stories.

Finally, her fascinated soul made her read that story. With great enthusiasm, she read the whole story for several hours without stopping. After reading, the events and characters of the story found a special place in her mind and soul as before, and she was reminded of film and acting again.

Immediately after reading the story, she realized that it could be a good subject for a film, and more importantly, that she could find some of the realities of her life in that story.

A few weeks had passed since her soul had been captivated by the story. After days and weeks of fighting with herself, she decided to write a screenplay based on it, and perhaps with Richard's help she could bring it to the screen. She managed to write the script with great interest and perseverance in a few weeks. Of course, she made changes in the story according to her own will and taste. She re-entered the world of film with great fascination, after which she went to see a plastic surgeon and underwent surgery on her neck and chest scars.

Roger and Sandra and her parents were delighted to see her return to life and art with so much enthusiasm. Of course, each of them, including Carol herself, was afraid of slipping back into the world of madness, but Carol's decision to have plastic surgery and her enthusiasm about returning to normal life made them all happy.

One evening, as Carol stared out the window of her room into the courtyard, she noticed Richard returning from a trip.

The next day she made a bouquet of diverse and beautiful flowers and went to the building where Richard lived, with the story and script. The housekeeper told her that Richard was still in his bedroom. Carol walked over to his bedroom and knocked on the door a few times.

"Who is it?" Richard said in a tired, sleepy voice. "Come in."

Carol entered the room with a beautiful smile. Richard, not expecting to see Carol in his room, sat up in his bed in embarrassment and stared at Carol. Carol first put the flowers in a vase and then said happily: "So your project is over?"

"Yes," said Richard, still quite surprised.

"I'm sure that beautiful girls and women accompanied you on that project," Carol said with a smile again.

Richard said with great surprise: "What do you mean?"

"Nothing, I just wanted to know if you are still single or not?"

Richard laughed and said: "Yes, no other woman has become part of my life yet."

Carol opened her scarf softly and, with a beautiful expression of joy and passion on her face, said: "What do you think?"

"Oh, I can't believe it, so you finally had surgery!" Richard said with great surprise and happiness. "But even with your scars, you were a very beautiful woman, but now you have become much more attractive." Then he paused and asked: "Can I ask you the reason for that? You always said that you don't want to destroy the effects of your injuries, what happened now?"

"Life goes on, I don't want to stay in my past memories anymore," Carol replied cheerfully.

"Oh, well, I had not seen such vivacity in you for a long time." Then he frowned and said: "I hope you are not playing a role again and that you really are happy and cheerful."

Carol laughed again and said: "No, rest assured, I'm not playing a role right now."

"You really surprised me," Richard said happily.

Carol took a serious look and said, "No, you haven't seen my real surprise yet. I'm getting ready for a new role."

"What? You are joking."

"No, I'm quite serious."

Then she handed the story and the script that she had put down next to the vase to Richard and said: "I received a story months ago and I have written a script based on that story and now I want you to read this story and the script, we should be able to make a film of it together."

"You have really surprised me now; I will do it willingly. Your re-entry into the cinema has already guaranteed the success of this film in advance. I do not believe it, are you sure?" said Richard, who was quite surprised. "Do you want to do this?"

"Of course, why do you think I put myself under the surgeon's knife? You'd better read this script first, I have not yet decided on the name of the story. Now not only can you direct this movie, but you can also play a role in it, you haven't acted in a movie in years."

"Yes," said Richard excitedly, "that's a very good idea. Given your presence and your return to the film, we will have no problem financing the film."

"But I prefer to do it independently, you can sell my house in another city."

"Well, whatever you say, I will be very happy to invest in the production of this film. Because I'm sure it will sell very well."

"You'd better read that story and script now."

122

"If you like the story and script, they cannot be bad and vulgar."

"I think we can start filming next year, of course, if you are hardworking and persistent."

"Yes, I will not accept any other work until this has been completed, and I promise to do my best to make it better."

***

It had been nearly a year and a half since Richard and Carol started preparing for the film, and they were set to begin filming early in the winter. Richard was busy providing the necessary facilities and conditions to produce the film, and Carol was immersed with all her soul and mind in the creation and development of her role in the film, and besides in various matters, she also helped Richard. The relationship between Carol and Richard became closer day by day and they were now partners. Richard hoped to be able to marry Carol after the film was made.

It was the beginning of winter when shooting began. Carol acted her scenes in the film with indescribable excitement. In addition to directing, Richard also acted in the film.

It was not until a few weeks into the winter that heavy snow fell and covered the ground with white. Now Carol was completely and deeply immersed in her role, a fictional character who reminded her again of the painful memories of her past. After the snow fell, Richard, along with other staff and filmmakers, began preparing for the scene of the car crash. During that time, Carol's mind and soul were again filled with horrific memories of the accident that had occurred in her real life.

Richard, who was working hard to produce the accident scene in the film, did not notice Carol's bad mood, and of course Carol tried hard to keep her bad mood a secret. Due to technical problems, the scene of the accident had to be re-shot several times, and its repetition was Carol's greatest mental torture. Every time she was in the car with two children and the actor who played her husband in the film, she remembered the scene of the accident and the death of her loved ones. It was very painful and torturous for her.

After filming that scene, she felt pain in her heart at night and was taken to the hospital.

Richard, who had just noticed Carol's distress, felt disgusted at himself. He should have realized earlier that doing some of the scenes in the film, especially the accident scene, would be hard work for Carol. He postponed filming until Carol fully recovered.

The first night that Carol was taken to the hospital, she fell asleep with painkillers, with a heart rate device monitoring her. In a dream, she saw again the caravan and the carriage with her husband and children in, and a snowman was driving the carriage. She was trying hard to get close to the carriage, when suddenly the snowman turned into a Roman soldier who had a whip on his hand. At that moment, her children cried and moaned and asked her to join the carriage, but she could not get close to the carriage no matter how hard she tried. She only saw her husband and children going away. She woke up at that moment, and while she was sweating and short of breath, she saw doctors and nurses rushing to get her heart rate back to normal.

After a while, a doctor came to her and said: "Fortunately, your heart rate has returned to normal, and you should sleep again." Sometime later, the doctor and nurses left her room so that she could sleep again, but after that nightmare, she could not sleep. So, she was only able to see her loved ones in anaesthesia, coma, and death.

The next morning, Richard entered the room with a bouquet of flowers, and after greeting, said sadly: "I blame myself for your situation, I am an idiot. I shouldn't have involved you in a film like this."

Carol replied indifferently: "No, you don't blame yourself at all, the production of this film was my own idea and request."

"Yes, but I should have been more careful when performing some scenes of the film. I was so immersed in my work that I did not notice your discomfort. You are also usually a master in your work of hiding your discomfort and not many people notice your aching soul and mind."

"It doesn't matter, we have filmed most parts of the story now and we have to start working again soon."

"I have postponed the filming for a few weeks and if necessary, I will postpone it again for a longer time, your health is more important than anything else."

"Don't worry, I will be released from the hospital in a few days and with a little rest we can start filming again, I just want you to change something."

"What?"

"The scene where I decided to commit suicide in that movie and you stop me from doing it by talking and expressing your love, do you know which scene I am talking about?"

"Yes of course."

"I'd like that scene to be the last scene we shoot."

After thinking for a while, Richard said in surprise: "That scene should not be a difficult scene for you, why do you want it to be the last scene?"

"You're wrong again," Carol said with a bit of anger: "You are wrong again, performing that scene is even more difficult for me than performing the scene of the accident, because it brings back memories, that scene would be better as the last scene, because I don't want our work to be postponed again because of my difficulty and sickness."

"You should not worry about the delay or the cost of producing this film, as I said, the most important thing is your health and recovery."

"Thank you, but as I said, I would like that scene to be the last one.

"Well, whatever you want."

***

Filming began again a few weeks after Carol was released from hospital. Richard noticed a noticeable change in Carol's behaviour and in their relationship. Although Carol was trying her best to look fresh and energetic, great sadness had taken over her whole mind and soul again. She resorted to alcohol to escape grief, and often secretly drank large amounts. Richard also noticed a change in her acting style.

One day a scene from the movie was supposed to be filmed, but Carol did not turn up. Richard immediately went to see her at her house to find out the reason for her absence but found her completely drunk. He approached her sadly and asked:

"What happened? Are you okay?"

Carol said with a smile: "Do you consider yourself a director? You still do not understand that I am completely drunk?"

"We were all waiting for you, is it a good time to get drunk?"

"Neither you nor anyone else has the right to question or control me," Carol replied angrily. "I appear in front of the camera whenever I want."

"But you cannot stand in front of any camera like this, you should not drink a lot because of your heart condition, I am more worried about your health than anything else."

"It's not up to you if I drink, this is just good for my acting and continuing this movie."

"What are you talking about? By doing so, you are only destroying yourself and increasing the cost of producing this film."

Carol stumbled up to him, stared at his face and said: "What do you expect from a mother who has lost her husband and children in real life? Are you waiting for her happiness, or are you witnessing her sadness and madness, which one?"

"Yes, in real life we will certainly see her suffering."

"I also intend to portray the same facts. After the accident, I must present a transformed face in this film, the audience will be able to understand and distinguish a happy, energetic and hopeful mother from a lost mother."

"You mean you want to improve your acting by drinking like this? I know you're a follower of Method Acting, but you're destroying yourself like this, I've concluded that we have to shut down, I don't want to see you die."

"No, we have to keep working, you know how important this is to me, I'm sorry I overdid the alcohol today, I promise it won't happen again." Then she threw herself into Richard's hands and said: "It's better to finish this movie as soon as possible, after that we will both need a long break, and most importantly we will be officially married. I'm counting the moments until that day, let's finish this as soon as possible.

***

Despite much frustration, Carol managed to complete the rest of the film, leaving only the final scene which was a big deal for her. Richard did not fully understand why that last scene was so difficult for Carol. Carol also hid her troubles with great skill and mastery. At Carol's request, filming of the final scene was postponed twice.

Richard who was upset told Carol: "We'd better cut that scene after all, this movie has had very beautiful and glorious scenes so far and we do not need to film that scene."

"No, it's a beautiful scene, and we have to do it," Carol replied sadly. "It's more valuable to me than just 'one scene.' I have been preparing for it for a long time."

At last, the promised day came. Carol stared sadly at the snow that had just settled on the ground.

Then went to Richard and said: "We only do this scene once. Do not interrupt the filming in any way in the middle of the scene. We do not need to follow the script exactly."

Richard shook his head and said: "Okay, whatever you say, but it's not too late. If this scene upsets you, we can ignore it."

"No, this will be the best part of this movie."

Mendoza, who was behind the scenes because of his interest in the film, took the opportunity to approach Carol and said happily: "I think this is your acting masterpiece, I have not seen you this powerful in any other films of yours."

Carol stared at Mendoza for a moment and then said: "I have to thank you for encouraging me back to the world of cinema with your beautiful story. We actors have nothing to show without a good story."

After arranging the filming, Richard came to Carol and said: "Okay, everything is ready. I have ordered several cameras to film the scene without interruption."

It was a scene where Carol had to stand on the roof of a tall building to throw herself down and commit suicide, but her lover, played by Richard, dissuaded her from doing so.

Before the cameras started, Carol hugged Richard tightly, and after kissing him with tears in her eyes, said: "Thank you for everything, I just have to say that when I told you, I love you and I want to marry you, I wasn't acting, that was my heartfelt reality."

Richard kissed her forehead and said in surprise: "Was it? You mean, it is not anymore, eh?"

"I still love you and you know it."

"Yes, I know you love me, now it's better to finish this damn scene as soon as possible, I cannot stand to see your sadness."

Staring at Richard, Carol gently and slowly approached the edge of the roof, pushed aside some of the snow, and stood on the edge of the roof.

"Be very careful," said Richard sadly. "It's slippery there. You'd better not move."

Carol was standing on the roof with a sad face, staring at the ground. Her soul was full of longing and the need to see and touch her loved ones, no, this time she would not allow the caravan and chariot to take her loved ones without her. She had to try again, maybe it was only death that connected her to her loved ones. Death, the same dazzling white light, the same ecstatic twist in the air, the same unparalleled serenity, the same glorious fluidity of water, the same feeling of touching and embracing her children, getting lost and freeing from pain and homesickness and nostalgia and facing a world of wonders. By throwing myself from this height, I will experience the frightening and deadly twists and turns in the air again, just like the twists and turns when the accident took place, and this time I will embrace death completely and become the lucky passenger of the caravan of happiness.

At that moment, she heard Richard's voice saying: "Hey, Carol, please look at me, what are you going to do?"

Carol looked down at the ground and stared at Richard with a sad, frightened face.

"Hey Carol, please come down from the edge of the roof."

Carol stared at Richard's face for a while, then said: "I've reached the end, did I say the end? No, I'm going to start another trip."

"What trip? Please come down."

"A journey in which I will be with my husband and children again."

"Carol, what do you want to do? You cannot be with your husband and children; they have been gone for a long time."

"No, they will never go without me, I was separated from them once in the world of death, but I will not allow anything or anyone to keep me away from them."

"Carol, please don't talk like this, you will not reach them by killing yourself, the force of death will not bind you to them."

"So what? Which force can connect me to them?"

"The power of love," Richard replied in tears. "With the power of love, you will have them by your side, and you will fill others with your love. I will help you in that way, you know that I love you, I have loved you for many years." Then he extended his hand and said: "Come and take my hand, let us start a new life, I love you and I admire your talent and beauty, you have no right to deprive me and others of that great and creative soul, please come and take my hand."

Carol, her face filled with tears, stared at Richard's sad face for a moment and said softly: "The power of love? What a sweet dream," and then closed her eyes and threw herself down. The horrible twists and turns had begun, she was light-headed and abandoned in the thought of joining the caravan of happiness. Near the first floor, Carol suddenly landed on a large rescue net. Richard, who had long predicted that Carol might commit suicide, had a large rescue net installed on the first floor of the building.

After landing on the rescue net, Carol opened her eyes in surprise, and after a few moments, she realized that she was on a rescue net and that people were trying to bring her down. She only felt pain in her shoulder and blood flowed from her nose. Richard immediately came down and put Carol in an ambulance and transported her to the hospital, where doctors and nurses quickly examined her, and again admitted her to a room where both her heart and her mental state could be checked.

The next day, Richard met her with a sad face and sat by her bed without saying a word and stared at her. Carol stared at Richard for a moment and then said: "Tell me something. Why are you looking at me like this?"

Richard replied sadly: "I am very sad and at the same time disappointed. I hoped that with my love I would stop you from doing that, but I could not, my love was not enough for you."

"I'm disappointed, too," Carol replied sadly.

"Disappointed with what?"

"You were right, they are gone, I am talking about my husband and my children, I could not feel their presence in those horrible and deadly twists, you are right they are gone."

"So, that madness of yours was at least as good as the fact that you now understand that they are gone, and you will not find them again with your suicide and death, hmm?"

"Now I have to live, but I had to try that way," Carol shook her head sadly.

"You deceived me again; I feel that you have played me again."

"No, not at all, as I said I did love you and I am in love with you, I just did not want to tell you my truth about that last scene." Then she laughed and said: "But I couldn't deceive you this time, you knew that I might throw myself from there."

Richard smiled and said: "I have been in this profession for many years, I am also able to understand the acting of others, of course, I must say about you that I can never be completely sure whether you are acting or are being truthful."

Carol smiled and opened her arms. She called Richard into her arms and hugged him tightly and said: "I swear this is real, I love you and if I was not connected to these machines, I would be kneeling in front of you and asking you to marry me: will you marry me?"

Richard kissed her passionately and with tears in his eyes said: "Yes, you are the woman of my dreams."

At the same time, there was knocking on the door of the room, and Carol said: "Come in."

Mendoza entered the room with a bouquet of flowers in his hand and stared at Carol in sadness, then said, "Are you alright?"

Carol smiled and said: "Yes, I'm fine." Then she turned to Richard and said, "Do you see what beautiful flowers Mendoza has brought me? It was as if you had forgotten to bring me a bouquet of flowers today." Then she opened her hands and asked Mendoza to hug her. Mendoza hugged Carol for a moment in embarrassment, and then said in surprise: "But in the story and in the script, you were not supposed to throw yourself from the top of that building."

"We had to change some parts," Carol replied with a smile.

"I have to say that it was a very powerful and very real scene, you are a very skilled and powerful actor."

Meanwhile, Richard smiled and said: "I have found a good name for this film."

Carol and Mendoza both asked: "What?"

Richard replied, "Carol played that last scene with all her might, and she actually played Death. No one else can play Death as much as she really did. So, the better name for the movie is "I played Death."

Mendoza shook his head happily and said, "Yes, this is the best title for the film."

After a while, Mendoza said goodbye to them, and as he was about to leave the room Carol first smiled and gave a mischievous look at Richard, then said: "Hey, Mendoza, do you have another story?"

End – Mark Hill (M.Ofogh)

08/08/10

footnotes:

(1) Margot Bickel: Silence full of the unspoken

(2) Samloo: Aida Memory of Tree and Dagger

(3) Margot Bickel: Silence full of the unspoken

Biography

Mark Hill a British citizen of Iranian origin, living in London. He was born on 1962 in Tehran. When he finished his high school (military high school) he entered to Army University and graduated as an army officer. He was forced to be in the war between Iran and Iraq for many years. He came to UK in 1989 as a refugee and since then he has managed to write 18 novels, several plays, and a collection of some poems, both in English and in Farsi. He has 2 degrees science from Army University of Iran and math with computer from a university in London.

Printed in Great Britain
by Amazon

18974851R00081